Road

Zombie Castle 2

Road

Chris Harris

PRESS

Published by DHP Publishing in 2018
This edition published by Vulpine Press in the United Kingdom in 2025

Cover by Vulpine Press
ISBN: 978-1-83919-610-2

www.vulpine-press.com

CHAPTER ONE

Twenty people and one baby sat on the roof eating their breakfast.

Maud had once again cobbled together a delicious meal from only camping stoves. The porridge and bannock bread cakes (flour and water mixed together with raisons, and then fried) were delicious and would give us all the energy we knew we needed to survive another day. Becky kept another camping stove going, boiling kettles of water to make the gallons of tea and coffee the adults seemed to need.

Sarah, the baby, now sleeping and oblivious to everything, was a great distraction for all of us. All of us preferring to gaze at the baby rather than the reality of the situation that was surrounding us twenty feet below.

The roof of the building we were on at Bickley Barracks outside Plymouth had provided us not only with new members for our group, but with shelter for the night. We knew we had to leave, and soon, but for the moment we were safe. And that extra cup of coffee would delay our facing the zombies below, whose only aim in life was to eat us, for just ten more minutes or so.

The calm was shattered by a shout from my son, Stanley. To keep the children occupied, as they had wolfed their breakfasts down in no time and didn't seem as reluctant as the adults to start the day, we had given them the task of being lookouts.

"There are more zombies coming."

The adults looked at each other ruefully and exchanged a few shrugs, knowing we could delay no longer. Standing up and stretching, I walked over to the edge of the roof with Sergeant Dave Eddy and Sergeant Simon Wood.

Two battle-scarred, tough as nails Marines who had fought alongside each other in many conflicts and who had been reunited yesterday. We now looked to them for their military expertise and fighting skills, which we were desperately going to need if we were to survive.

While everyone else worked together to finish packing the gear we'd transferred up to the roof to make our overnight stop as comfortable as possible, the three of us stood beside the children and stared at the approaching zombies.

Despite the fact we'd thinned out the zombies that had over-run the base, about fifty still surrounded the building we were standing on, their low groans and rasping breath the only noise they made as they coalesced into one group, waiting, just waiting for the next meal to appear. As far as we could see in all directions, lay the efforts of our labours yesterday. Hundreds of corpses lay scattered in droves, killed for a second time by us either running them over and crushing them with our vehicles, or by stabbing them through the brain with our improvised zombie spears. A few had been shot as we had familiarized ourselves with the various weapons we now had, but the need to conserve ammunition had kept that number down, as they posed no danger to us on the roof and we knew that once we were back in our vehicles, we could easily kill them. Looking at the approaching, staggering crowd, Simon said.

"I reckon there's at least another hundred coming our way."

"Where are they coming from?" Dave asked, to no one in particular. Thinking for a few moments I replied, "We know they're attracted by noise, so they've probably been following our little convoy, or are just attracted by all the noise we've been making.

There's not much else to distract them, so they keep heading to whatever grabs their attention and keep going until they find it."

I gave a grim laugh.

"I'm sounding like an expert, but it's what happens on the TV shows and it makes a kind of sense. We ain't never going to get away from them, we'll always be the noisiest thing around, with the tractor and car and all the shooting we've been doing. They'll always catch up with us eventually."

Dave stood quietly for a moment, arms crossed, with one hand supporting his chin. You could almost hear his mind working as he contemplated the scene in front of him. More zombies came into view, following the lead pack.

"Right, then," he said, turning to face and address us all. His low voice, though quiet, easily reached us all.

"Small change of plan. Let's get packed and back in the vehicles. We may as well all load up and go together to scavenge what other supplies we can. There's no point coming back here again, we just need to get what we can and go. By the look of it, there are a lot more of them heading our way, so splitting up is not an option anymore."

Initially the plan had been to leave a group on the roof, while a group toured the base, scavenging whatever we could find.

Turning to the children, Dave said in his best Sergeant's voice, "Well done, Marines. We're all going to need your young eyes to keep us safe." Pointing at Stanley, my son, he continued, "And you, young man. I've heard all about you and your skills with a cricket bat. You must show me how to do that. You are one brave Marine."

Stanley beamed with pleasure. I nodded at Dave, who winked at me.

While the children had slept last night, one of the topics of conversation had been how to deal with and protect the children from the horrors they had already seen, and what they would no doubt witness daily from now on.

The universal agreement was that we would all obviously protect every child with our own lives if need be. But there was no way we could stop them seeing and experiencing the reality of the lives we were now living.

Even though we would always be the first to fight to protect them, it was essential they be able to defend themselves if need be. Daisy, my little baby girl, already carried a knife in a sheath on her belt, and Stanley his zombie-killing cricket bat. Eddie had claimed a zombie spear, which was never far from his grasp.

As to the new junior members of our group, Emma, at six, was too young to really do anything but run. But Josh, who was twelve, would be able to wield a weapon if need be.

Simon and Dave had both said that once the opportunity arose, they would begin training us all, including the children, in military tactics and fighting techniques. Everyone, they said, could play a part, including Emma, who could be shown how to reload magazines with bullets. In battle a supply of freshly loaded magazines could mean the difference between life and death.

They did add that first they would both have to learn from us how to kill a zombie up close and personal with a knife, as they hadn't dared do it yet, and after Shawn's and my demonstration the day before at the Armoury, they realized guns were not the only answer.

I looked around. It was a hive of activity as the last few items were gathered and passed down into the trailer.

Becky was supervising the loading and Shawn was putting the last few items into the subfloor we'd created. Noah, Daniel and Aggie were holding a demonstration on how to use the zombie spears for those who had not used them yesterday, while Maud was looking after Sarah and keeping a general eye on the children.

Maud looked frail and gentle, holding little Sarah.

"I don't care if you don't want to go. You all need to go to the toilet before we leave. We are not stopping every five minutes because one of you needs the toilet," she said, as she herded the children in the general direction of the toilet we had constructed.

I chuckled when I heard her, as others around me did. How many millions of times had parents issued the same instructions to children before a long car journey? It now had a different meaning. She could have said, "Children, we are not stopping or getting out of the car to go to the toilet, because you will get eaten by that zombie over there."

It did remind me though, that I had better go as well before we left!

CHAPTER TWO

Just before we started our engines, I stood up on the seat of my car and got everyone's attention.

"Right, we all know who is doing what. Things can change, so remember that Simon's in charge of the trailer, and I am of the Volvo. So, if we say something, just bloody do it."

Everyone nodded and looked deadly serious,

My Eisenhower-esque dawn of war speech concluded, I sat down and started the engine.

Dave had taken Ben's seat next to me in the Volvo, while Chet and Steve the Marine stood up on my back seats, leaning against the side of the hole that had once been a roof, with their weapons held ready. Steve had his SA80 and sidearm; Chet had chosen one of the pump-action shotguns we'd recovered from the Armoury.

Louise was riding in the cab of the tractor with Shawn, armed with a shotgun to provide another pair of eyes and extra protection for Shawn.

With spears in the other hand and boxes of ammunition and shotgun cartridges stacked on the seat between them, everyone braced themselves as I followed the tractor and bumped over the corpses I couldn't dodge.

The tractor, with its zombie plough on the front, pushed the living dead out of the way, or mangled them enough so they slipped under the blade of the plough for our tyres to bump over, while eight adults in the trailer stabbed with their spears at any other zombie that was near enough as they slowly passed them.

Chet, Steve and Dave in my car did the same to any that had got close to us.

The plan we had come up with was to stop at various places around the base, including the shop and vehicle repair area, where we could gather useful supplies and equipment. We would also stop at places where there should be quantities of ammunition stored. Moving between these locations, we would also keep an eye out for weapons lying abandoned on the ground, and on or near dead former comrades in arms.

That was why we had three in my car. When a weapon or something else useful was spotted, probably by either Shawn, who was driving the tractor and so had a clear view of what was in front, or from someone from the vantage point of the high trailer, a call over the radio or a shout and a wave from the trailer would warn us. I would then stop, and Chet and Steve would jump out via the roof of my car, and covered by myself and Dave with our weapons, they would retrieve whatever the item was and pass it up to us in the car.

While we were doing that, Shawn would circle round and keep any approaching zombies at bay. A plan we had not tested yet.

Shawn's voice came through the radio. "Guns coming up on the right."

I spotted the grizzly remains of three soldiers lying on the ground. From what I could make out, they'd died with their backs to each other, trying to fight off a horde of zombies that had surrounded them. They'd not died cheaply, and all around them lay the carcasses of those they'd killed before being overpowered.

One of the Marine's bodies, even though it looked as if had been passed through a blender, was moving. He'd turned before death could find him, but his body was so destroyed, all it could do was jerk spasmodically.

As Chet and Steve climbed down from the roof, Dave called softly to them from beside me.

"Don't hesitate, boys. Steve, you know the Marine on the floor. Send him to his mates. He'll thank you for it. But first, be careful of the ones you're stepping over, they may not be dead yet."

We watched as they carefully walked the few paces through the bodies, circling the soldiers, and delivering the occasional stab through the head with a spear to ones they were not sure were dead.

Steve paused and while Chet stood back, he mouthed a few silent words to his brother-in-arms, before delivering his final duty.

"Good lad," Dave said, "Now, don't fuck about, grab what you can and get your arse back in the car, we ain't got all day." Motivation, military style!

While they stripped the corpses of their rifles and any magazines they had, Shawn had driven in a circle, and was driving at and through the zombies following us. No matter how many he kept re-killing, more seemed to keep coming.

Watching as they struggled back with their load, I realized that a bag would have made their job easier. As they handed the haul up to us and climbed up themselves, I shouted up to Becky in the trailer to find a bag we could use next time.

In total, we stopped six times to strip weapons and ammunition from corpses on our way through the base, the luggage area on my car now almost overflowing with hastily thrown in weapons.

At the base shop after everyone apart from Maud and the children had climbed down from the trailer to help, both Shawn and I used our vehicles to defend us from the ever-closer approaching horde, while they emptied the shelves and the storeroom and stacked them outside, ready for loading.

We had underestimated how long it would take to empty the shop and its storeroom, and the approaching zombies, despite our best efforts, continued to get closer and grow in numbers. We needed to gather as much food as we could, so abandoning what was still there was an option we'd already agreed we didn't want to take unless absolutely necessary.

Simon and Dave, knowing this and realizing the situation could get out of control very quickly, ordered an immediate change of tactics.

Over the radios he ordered Shawn and me to line our vehicles up as a physical shield to protect the ones emptying the shelves and storeroom of the shop. As we approached, he directed us where to stop.

Chet and I got out of the car and steadied our weapons on the metal sheets surrounding my vehicle. They were dented and streaked in blood and gore, but had stood up brilliantly to the punishment they had received. Last night Shawn had told us about improvements he wanted to make to both vehicles when he had the time and equipment. They'd both passed their 'baptism of fire' with flying colours, but improvements could always be made.

Dave told Steve, Jim and Shawn to climb up into the trailer.

We formed a firing line. I had my shotgun and my .22 rifle.

"Take your time and pick your shots," Simon shouted, "Keep talking to each other and for fuck's sake, keep your eyes on a swivel and calling targets."

The seven of us steadied our weapons and took aim. A few seconds later Simon shouted, "This is not Waterloo. You can see the enemy. You don't need my permission to discharge your weapon. Kill them all!"

Despite the situation, I found myself chuckling at the endless phrases that both Simon and Dave must have gathered during their years as Sergeants. Single shots rang out as we all fired carefully at the approaching herd. In no time I had emptied one magazine. Ejecting it, I reached into my pocket to grab and insert the next one, and charged the rifle so it was ready to fire. I was pleased that from ten shots I'd felled eight zombies, but was aware that I only had one more loaded magazine in my pocket.

The continual and accurate fire from the four trained soldiers was mowing down the zombies. Chet, realising his shotgun didn't have the range to do any damage, had grabbed an SA80. Having only fired the weapon for the first time yesterday, he wasn't as consistent, but occasional cries of 'Yes' were a testament to his growing accuracy.

By the time I was halfway through my third and final magazine, all the ones within effective range had been killed. More were coming, but Simon shouted,

"Cease fire! Let them get closer, it's a waste of ammo trying to get a headshot that far out."

Becky shouted to get my attention, waving at the pile of mainly food they had cleared from the shop. "That's about it. Can we start to load up now?"

Glancing at Simon, who nodded, I replied, "Yes. Let's form a chain and get this on board now. Simon, if you and Dave continue to cover us, can everyone else help?"

"Yes, we can cover this, mate," Simon replied, "If we need help, you ain't exactly far away, are you?" he said, pointing at the pile of goods only five metres away. "Steve, go and muck in. Jim, before you go, give Simon and me a hand to reload the mags."

While the trailer filled with goods, Jim and Dave gathered up the ejected magazines, and, opening one of the ammunition cans, reloaded all the used magazines.

Soon everything was on board, and the increasing level of fire from our guards an urgent and compelling indication it was time to leave. Wasting no time, we all quickly went to our original places in the vehicles and slowly pulled away.

Dave shouted across to us, "I'll direct Shawn to the mechanics' workshop and then unless we see anything else of use, the only other place we should stop at is the guard house. We can't have enough ammo, and we're burning through it at a fair rate. I hope we can get some more there."

No matter how many we killed, two more seemed to replace each one. I had no idea where they were coming from, but they kept coming. They were a mix of all ages and sexes, so they were most probably just locals attracted by whatever noise we were making. The crack of high-powered rifles and the boom of shot-guns were the obvious culprits, but what else were we to do?

It was a catch 22 situation. The gunfire was attracting them in their droves, but the only way to protect ourselves from the sheer number of them was to use the guns, which kept them coming. We needed to change our tactics when we moved on, but for now they were keeping us safe, so we had to carry on.

We were still twenty-one.

CHAPTER THREE

The vehicle maintenance area proved to be a treasure trove of equipment. There was too much available for us to carry, so Shawn and I made snap decisions and indicated what we should take. The heaviest item was a portable generator, which took six of us to manhandle into the trailer.

An urgent shout from Simon, who with Steve was providing protection, drew our attention to the horde of zombies they were failing to keep at bay, despite their sustained and accurate marksmanship.

"We need to go right now!"

As soon as this command was issued, without hesitation everyone rushed to their vehicle and within thirty seconds we were all on board and ready to go.

The base was huge. Dave had given Shawn a hastily drawn map showing the quickest route to the main entrance gate we'd entered though yesterday. As the volume of zombies increased, all ideas of gathering more equipment from other places were abandoned. Shawn was having to weave the tractor to pick the easiest route through the masses heading towards us.

Shawn, rounding a corner, stopped so suddenly that I almost ran into the back of him, the shouts of protest and alarm I could hear indicating that none of his passengers were ready for the sudden stop.

One by one, I could see them all reappearing as they picked themselves up from the bed of the trailer.

The way ahead was blocked by a sea of stumbling undead. The route we were taking to the main exit from the base narrowed between a long line of buildings, compressing the bodies into a solid mass. An uncountable number of zombies blocked our way.

The panic was evident in Shawn's voice as his question came through the walkie talkie.

"Is there another way? I'm not sure if I can get through this." Dave picked up the radio.

"There's a turning on the left in about a hundred yards. If you carry on you should soon see it. There are a few fences in the way, but it'll take us to the sports fields. It's a straight run to the gate-house from there."

Quickly judging the distance, it was going to be a close-run thing who would get to the turning first. Us or the undead.

Shawn, realising this as the same time I did, slammed his foot on the accelerator and the tractor took off like a rocket. I couldn't help but smile as about half of the occupants of the trailer, the ones who didn't have a good strong grip, disappeared, as for the second time in less than a minute they were sent flying by the sudden and unexpected move.

"Hold on!" I shouted the unnecessary warning to the passengers as they were all already clinging on for dear life, as I too accelerated rapidly, trying to keep as close as I could to the rear of the trailer as it surged up the road.

My view ahead was blocked by the trailer, so I was relying on the odd shouted warning from Dave, who was leaning out of the roof as far as he dared to grab glimpses of the route ahead.

The bangs and thumps grew from the car as it bounced violently over the mangled corpses left by the tractor that I did not have time to avoid, given how closely I was following it.

I could hear the tractor's engine roaring louder as Shawn changed down through the gears to give the tractor the power it needed to ram through and destroy the multitude we were facing, its speed dropping as he did so.

We had clearly lost the race to the turning. I slowed, matching Shawn's reducing speed, trying to keep as close as I could to the trailer. The sight out through the windows was terrifying. Our small convoy had pushed deep into the zombies. Compressed by the buildings, the concentrated crowd directed all their attention towards us, arms trying to reach us over the metal sides that had felt impenetrable so far, but now felt weak and insufficient.

Before, we had been moving when we'd encountered crowds of the undead, so speed had been our friend, not enabling them to get too close to us.

Dave, Tom and Chet were shouting, screaming and swearing as they used their spears to destroy the brains of any zombie they could reach.

Dave was shouting loudest of all, his battle cries keeping everyone's killing frenzy going. The tractor had slowed to a crawl.

"His wheels are spinning!" Dave screamed at me, "Too many bodies under the wheels, he's losing traction."

"Shit!" I screamed, my mind racing.

A zombie, somehow pushed by the others, was almost over the wedge at the front of my vehicle. His teeth snapping as it looked at me with dark eyes, the primeval look on its face showed its desire to reach me, to pass on the infection. The virus needed to spread to survive. It would not rest until the entire human race had succumbed. I was almost paralysed with fear at the intent to kill me shown on the face of a zombie who was bizarrely dressed only in swimming trunks.

A day or so ago, he'd been just a normal man, most likely on holiday with his family. Now he was a hideous creature, half of his face torn off, whose only aim in life was to end mine.

I couldn't see ahead, but I could imagine the wheels of the tractor spinning as they lost purchase on the soft bodies of the ones it was running over, only finding grip when the heavy duty tyres ripped apart the body, until they reached tarmac and got enough grip to push the vehicle forward until the next one halted progress.

Dave reached forward and ended the swimming trunk-clad zombie's existence with a single thrust of the spear through its head.

"We need to do something, it's getting a bit sporty out here," he said, stating the obvious, but his use of the phrase from one of my favourite war films calmed me down. I smiled and promised to myself that if we lived through this, I'd acknowledge Dave's recollection of it.

The zombies were getting closer. Standing on the bodies of their recently re-deceased comrades, they were close enough to claw against the car windows.

The tractor had stopped again and I could hear the engine revving as Shawn desperately tried to keep moving.

In desperation, everyone dropped their spears and began firing into the crowd.

At such close range, heads were exploding when hit by burst of high-velocity bullets from the soldiers' guns. The shotguns were turning faces into masses of singed meat and bone. But still they kept coming.

Not knowing what else to do, I crushed three more zombies against the back of the trailer. They'd been climbing on the bodies of others and were almost over the front of my car. Panicking and not in full control, I hit the rear of the trailer with more force than necessary.

The trailer moved! Me hitting it had given it enough force to move it forward slightly.

Dave saw this too and screamed, "Again!"

The wood and steel sheets that we had fixed to protect the sides of the trailer and to keep the wheels clear, provided a flat surface for me to push against. Trying to weigh the difference between ramming the car into the trailer and doing some terminal damage, which would not help our situation, and using enough force to help, I drove the car into the back of the trailer. The wedge at the front of the car buckled and crumpled.

It worked. The trailer moved another foot. Keeping the car against the trailer, I pressed the accelerator and increased the power. The engine screamed in protest and the wheels kept spinning as the Volvo fought the immense weight it was trying to push.

It worked. Slowly, ever so slowly, my car gave the tractor just the extra help it needed.

Even over the roar of both engines you could hear everyone screaming and cheering, willing our little convoy onward. The more momentum we gained, the easier it got, until soon I was not pushing the trailer but trying to keep up with it. I kept pressed against it, but that was more from not wanting to change what was obviously working.

Not being able to see anything other than the rear of the trailer, I was taken by surprise when it suddenly veered left. We had made the turning. The swearing and shouts of pain from my passengers as I turned sharply to keep close to the trailer indicated they too had been taken by surprise and were being thrown around.

The cries of alarm soon changed to cheers and shouts and screams of joy as we burst through a wooden fence and onto the sports field, leaving the zombies behind. Breathing a massive sigh of relief, I pulled back from the trailer and veered to the side. Seeing the way ahead was clear, I pulled up alongside the tractor.

Shawn waved his arm to indicate we should stop.

Parking up, I stood up on my seat and waved stupidly at Becky and the kids. Everyone had a look of numb, shocked relief on their faces. I could also hear Sarah wailing her protest at the rough ride and noise she'd had to endure.

After a quick check we were all ok, we agreed to keep moving and leave the base and find somewhere to stop once we were clear. No one disagreed, as the mass of zombies was now visible again and heading our way.

Before I moved off, I stared long and hard at the approaching horde. Their pursuit was relentless. For the last few days we had run from them, fought them, killed them in their droves, but still they came. No matter how many we destroyed, more took their place. The depressing reality was that we could outpace them in the short term, but they would catch us up, or others would find us first.

We needed to get to our castle, and soon. How much more could we take before our luck ran out?

CHAPTER FOUR

The guardhouse at the gate entrance yielded another good supply of arms and ammunition, which we wasted no time stacking in the boot of the Volvo.

Before we set off, Dave got Steve and Chet to close the gates to the base and secure them.

"There must be thousands still in there. The only way in or out should be this gate so if we lock it, then it's a few less for us to worry about and it could help others trying to survive around here." His reasoning and logic sound, we congratulated him and set off north.

The previous night we had mapped the route we thought would be best. The plan was to take as many side roads as possible and reach Dartmoor. The distance wasn't far, just a few miles as the crow flies. Dartmoor was one of the last true wildernesses left in the south of England. A vast area of moorlands, forests, rivers and tors or rock formations. We anticipated its low population and few towns and villages would make it a fairly zombie-free area, and so provide a safe route.

Our hope would have been to get past Dartmoor and via the main A38, reach the M5 motorway before we called a halt for the day. We would then try and use the three-lane motorway as the fastest route north towards our goal of trying to find and rescue the friends and families of our little band. It had the advantage that it would be wide enough for us to turn around and find another route if we found the way blocked.

But glancing at the time, I realised that it was already past midday. Dave and Simon had insisted that we needed to find a place to spend the night by at least four o'clock. This, they explained, would give us enough time to improve the security of our accommodation, if necessary.

It would also enable us to carry out any cooking, repairs or modifications we needed to make while we still had daylight. If we could manage without the need for illumination, we might avoid any unwanted attention.

The crushed front wedge on my Volvo certainly needed some attention. It had saved us, but it needed fixing if it was going to stand up to any more abuse.

Driving slowly down a B road, we headed towards Dartmoor, Shawn occasionally slowing to shunt a vehicle out of the way or for us to dispatch single or small groups of zombies. We all kept our eyes peeled for danger or maybe other survivors. The few houses or small villages we passed were eerily quiet, with no signs of life, only the undead attracted to our small convoy.

We talked between ourselves, amazed at how quickly the country must have been infected. People had fled larger areas of population to escape outbreaks, but it was most likely that the plague had started in their area, and so they had unwittingly taken the disease with them, spreading it so quickly that any plan to contain it could have never have succeeded.

Globally by now, not one corner of the planet had escaped the rapid spread of the virus. It was just too perfect not to succeed. Our planet, due to the rapid advances in how we travel, had been called 'a global village'. Mankind was now paying the price of that progress.

But we had survived, so there must be others. Yes, we were in a sparsely populated area of the country, but all we were coming across was the undead.

In the trailer I could see Becky staring behind us, back the way we had come. Stopping at a junction, I stood on my seat to stretch my legs and, leaning on the roof, asked why she was looking behind us.

"If anyone was hiding in a house, we would be past and gone by the time they could do anything about it. They can see we're not moving that fast and so they might try and run after us. I just don't want to miss anyone, that's all."

"Keep looking, darling. We're going to need everybody we can find if we're going to get through this."

Dave had finished looking at the map by now, and via the radio, gave Shawn directions that would lead us towards Princetown, the small village at the heart of Dartmoor, and home to the famous prison.

"We should be there in an hour or so. It'll then be about time for us to start looking for a place to spend the night. I have a few in mind from the months I've spent crawling all over the sodding place on exercises. There's a farmhouse I know that's in the middle of absolutely bugger all, so it should be perfect. The farmer's a lovely chap, he used to let us sneak in and have a cup of tea and a warm by the fire.

Simon joined him. "Oh him! He is great. Ex-forces, Scottish and he always knew the value of a good brew and a warm up when the brass wasn't watching. The fact that all farmers have instructions not to offer us any assistance meant nothing to him. About ten years ago me and my boys spent a lovely night drinking whisky and eating good food when the weather turned shit on one crappy three-day training ex," he chuckled.

"I remember getting a pat on the back from the CO because we were the only unit to complete the mission. All the others bailed due to hypothermia and exposure. It turns out he knew what we'd done anyway. A few weeks after that, I drove up to drop him a couple of bottles of whisky off as a thank you, but the CO had beaten me to it. It turns out when Burgum was a lowly Lieutenant, he'd done the same thing himself a few times.

He showed me the note that arrived with the case of whisky, thanking him for NOT looking after his men when they most needed it." He slapped the side of the trailer.

"That settles it, we're heading to Willie Beedie's farm. If anyone's survived this shit, he will have."

We slowly moved onwards. Smoke could be seen rising from Princetown long before we reached it. We all exchanged silent looks and tensed, getting ready for the inevitable. I picked up the radio.

"Shawn, stop here and let me reconnoitre ahead. Dave says the road narrows through the village and if it's gridlocked, you'll have a hard time reversing or turning around. I'll nip ahead and check it out."

"Ok, buddy, be careful."

The mess of cars started over a mile from the village. A few zombies were staggering about and more were still trapped in their vehicles. Other cars had piled into each other or into walls and ditches in the now familiar scene of complete chaos and carnage we had seen before, and which we were certainly going to keep seeing every day of our journey.

A few glimmers of hope were vehicle tracks that we could see going away from the road across fields and off into the moor. Four-by-four owners with cars that had probably only been over speed bumps before had suddenly realised the value of high ground-clearance and the off-road capabilities of their pride and joy, and they had used it to enable them to survive.

I weaved carefully through the cars, with Dave, Chet or Steve destroying the brains of any zombie within reach, until eventually the way was completely blocked with a huge crush of cars, most containing the now familiar jerking movements of occupants still trapped by seat belts.

Dave climbed out of the car, stood on the bonnet and surveyed the way ahead through binoculars. A few minutes later he climbed back in and sat down.

"Better turn around. The centre of the village is swarming with them, most of the buildings seem to have burnt out and a few have collapsed completely, blocking any way through. It looks freaking awful up there. Jesus, if that's one little village, what the hell do towns and cities look like?"

He reached for the map.

"Give me a few minutes and I'll work out the best route to Willie's farm."

While he studied the map, I turned the Volvo around, adding a few more dents to its anti-zombie protection, and drove back to where the others were waiting. Pulling up beside the tractor, Dave gave them a quick résumé of what lay ahead. After getting a bearing on his compass and rechecking the map, he pointed in a direction.

"Willie's farm is about five miles that way."

We looked across the vast expanse of the barren moor. Small copses of trees lay in sheltered folds of the land and high granite tors dominated the landscape.

Shawn and Louise had exited the cab and were standing on the high wheel arches of the tractor.

"Tom, you follow me, because this tractor should be able to go anywhere within reason. If you stay close to me, I'll be able to pull you through if you get stuck."

I studied more closely the direction we planned to head towards. Footpaths crossed the moors, going in all directions, thousands of boots over the decades compacting the ground, marking clear routes over the moor.

"If we can stick to those paths as much as possible, I should be fine. The Volvo's got a good four-wheel drive system, it's just the ground clearance that might let it down."

Simon chipped in, "Give me a good old Defender any day. They'll go anywhere you point 'em. You may as well hook it up to the tractor now, Shawn, his Chelsea Tractor will be bogged down within one hundred yards."

Smirking, I responded, "Bloody purist, give it a chance, you might be surprised at what it can do." Becky joined in.

"He wanted to get a Defender as the family runabout. Tom made me take one for a test drive, and it scared the life out of me. The thing had a mind of its own and just wanted to keep killing me at every bend and junction."

"Oh, Becky, I kept telling you, you needed to drive it, not *it* you. You can't let your guard down or be mean to one, or it'll have you. But yes, dear, you are right, the Volvo is much more comfortable to drive, and it's got aircon and heated seats, I know. Bet you wish we had one now, though, don't you?"

"'Good for a zombie apocalypse' was not on the wish list at the time, though, was it, Tom? And if you've all finished slagging off my lovely safe family vehicle, can we get a move on? We've got zombies pouring out of that village and heading towards us."

Looking towards Princetown, she was right. You could faintly make out the dark moving shape of a horde. The noise of my vehicle must have attracted them.

"We need to get out of sight of those, or they'll follow us across the moor." I climbed back into my seat and started the engine.

"Hang on a mo," shouted Chet, "I have an idea that might distract them."

He scrambled out of the roof and ran up to the trailer and asked for something. A minute later a 5-litre plastic petrol can was passed down to him. He walked up to the nearest car, lying abandoned with its door open, its occupants choosing to flee from the terror around them.

Whether they'd made it or not was anyone's guess.

Chet opened the can and soaked the inside of the vehicle with petrol. Shawn and I, realising what he was up to, had already moved our vehicle away from the car. He then laid a trail of petrol from the car and, looking around to check we were clear, bent down with a lighter and lit the fuel.

The yellow flame shot along the line and with a whoosh, the car burst into a huge fireball. Carrying the can, he ran to my car and scrambled back in through the roof. Looking at him, he had a huge grin on his face.

"I've always wanted to do that!"

The black smoke billowing from the burning vehicle was drifting towards Princetown. His hairbrained plan was going to work. We now had a smoke screen to hide our escape. A tyre exploded loudly. In my rear-view mirror, I could see Chet hopping up and down with excitement, admiring his handiwork.

We set out across the moor, making our own trail across the wilderness. Shawn slowed to a virtual crawl. The trailer had no suspension and the rough ground was throwing the occupants around. I could only see Noah and Victoria clinging on to the sides for support as it rolled and bounced over the rough terrain. I expected the rest had decided to sit on the cushions on the deck and hold on.

I had to tell Chet to sit down in his seat when a particularly bad hole I'd gone into almost threw him out of the car. Steve grabbing at his belt had saved him from going overboard. The route that had looked smooth from the road was passable, but it didn't make for a comfortable ride. I stuck close to Shawn and trusted him to find the best route for us.

The Volvo did great, it kept going, fording a few small streams and bouncing over rocks and dips I never thought it would have managed.

Dave had the map and kept Shawn updated on the rough direction he wanted him to head in. We were in the middle of nowhere, and the pall of smoke from the burning car had long ago disappeared over the horizon. Dartmoor ponies, the small, sturdy indigenous horses that are unique to this area and are allowed to live semi-wild on the moor, watched us with quizzing eyes as we slowly passed them.

"Willie's farm is in the next hollow. If we keep on in this direction, we'll cross the drive leading to it."

My stomach was beginning to complain about the lack of food. We had last eaten at breakfast and that seemed a long time ago now. I was briefly jealous of everyone in the trailer, because I was sure Maud was still providing endless snacks and titbits for anyone who wanted them, but looking at how uncomfortable it must be, I wasn't that jealous.

Dave's navigation was spot on, because after another uncomfortable and tiring twenty minutes of driving, we came to an unpaved road that led further into the depths of the moor.

"Shawn, turn left. You'll come to a gate in about half a mile and his farm is about another half a mile beyond that."

As soon as we were on the track, the going got a lot smoother and Shawn picked up the pace. Soon, faces began to appear looking over the side of the trailer. I chuckled to myself as they all looked decidedly green. Maybe they hadn't been eating any food after all.

Shawn slowed and stopped at a long wall that stretched into the distance, where the track was wide enough for me to pull alongside him. Dave stood up on the seat.

"I'll get the gate, ladies, can't have you lot doing all the work, can we?" He climbed out through the roof and jumped down. I nodded in approval as everyone assumed a lookout position. The team was coming together nicely.

As soon as Dave touched the gate to open it, a voice called from seemingly nowhere.

"Touch that gate and I will blow your fucking head off. Now kindly turn around and fuck off."

We all tensed and raised our weapons.

Dave, calm as ever, nonchalantly leaned against the gate and crossed his legs.

"Afternoon, Willie. Is that any way to greet friends? You remember me, I'm Sergeant Dave Eddy, Royal Marines and in the trailer is that big ugly bastard, Sergeant Simon Wood. We've all sat in your kitchen sharing tea, whisky and war stories. We just need the usual, if it's ok. Somewhere to shelter for the night and we'll be on our way tomorrow. If you have whisky, that will be a bonus, but I'm sure I can rustle up a few bottles from our supplies if you're running low."

The bush ten feet in front of him rustled, and a man appeared wearing full camouflage. He was holding a pump action shotgun.

"Are you accusing me of being stingy with ma whisky?" he said in a virtually unintelligible Scottish accent.

"Willie, you are Scottish, so of course you're as tight as a duck's arsehole. All I was saying was that we have our own whisky to share with you, if you feel we're imposing on your legendary hospitality too much."

With that, he laughed, reached into his pocket and pulled out a crumpled cigar, lit it with a Zippo and said,

"Well you'd better come in then. Pull into the yard. I just need to re-set up the security I dismantled when I saw you coming." Dave smiled.

"You knew it was me."

"Of course, well not you exactly, ma eyesight ain't that good, but I saw the uniforms in the trailer and sticking out the roof

29

of that bastardised car of yours, so I guessed you knew where I was, which means I've met you before. And if you're coming here, you must be in real shit, especially as you're not in service vehicles.

I've been watching you approach for the past half an hour. I just couldn't let you open ma gate without asking, now, could I?"

"Need a hand?"

"No, but I could do with someone to talk to while I'm doing it. All I've had to go on so far, about what the fuck's happening is the news before they stopped broadcasting, and conversations with other ham radio users around the globe. But they're getting fewer and fewer every day."

He turned to the rest of us, who were all listening intently to the conversation.

"If ya all just head up to ma house, park in the yard and get yourselves comfortable in the kitchen, me and young Davey here won't be long."

He opened the gate and we drove through and followed the track to the farmhouse we could just see the roof of in the distance.

We were now, even if temporarily, twenty-two.

CHAPTER FIVE

The farm was very picturesque, hidden in a valley and surrounded by a little woodland. The pretty farmhouse had a yard that was surrounded by barns and storage sheds. It was all very neat and tidy.

With Steve steadying the ladder, Chet and I helped everyone climb down from the trailer. After hugging Becky and the kids, we all stood around, unsure of what to do next. Maud spoke up.

"Well, he did say to make ourselves comfortable in the house. I don't know about you, but that's where I'm going."

"Yes, lets," said Becky.

"Tom, the kids could do with a run about to stretch their legs and let off some steam. If you could keep an eye on them?"

Victoria and Lucy said they would help me keep an eye on them as the rest trooped into the house. I had a quick check around to make sure it was safe and zombie-free, and then gave the children, after what we had been through in the last few days, a probably unnecessary quick reminder about just staying in the yard and never leaving our sight.

Stan, Daisy, Eddie, Emma and Josh were soon bombing around the yard playing tig, seemingly without a care in the world. It was great to watch, a break from the horrors of the outside world.

I chatted with Victoria and Lucy. They were both putting a very brave face on how they must truly be feeling. Within the last forty-eight hours they had lost their husbands, faced certain death along with their children, trapped on a roof of a building and then even when rescued by us, had endured the terror of almost getting overrun by the undead when we were trying to leave the base.

I'd heard that Army wives were by nature made of stern stuff, as their husbands spend so much time deployed facing constant dangers every day, or training, and so the women have to get on with it by themselves. Well, they certainly were living up to the reputation.

I had seen them wielding the zombie spears, fighting alongside everyone in the trailer. They hadn't taken a step back and let others do the fighting, as some women might, but had joined in. As far as I was concerned, they were already valuable members of our group.

They were taking obvious joy in seeing their children playing, forgetting for the moment the world outside the small yard.

Dave and Willie walked into the yard a short while later. Dave formally introduced us, and I shook the former soldier's hand and thank him profusely for letting us onto his property.

Dave had told me the little he knew about Willie while we were driving over the moors.

He had settled on the moors after leaving the Army, lived alone and kept himself to himself. Like most former soldiers, he wasn't open about his time in service, but from the few conversations between them and usually when deep into a bottle of whisky, he had opened up a little. He had fought in quite a few conflicts and had been to a lot of places around the world during his time in the Army. Dave said that his former CO had great respect for the man, which was enough for him.

Willie looked to be in his sixties, but with his face weathered by so many years on the moors, it was difficult to be exact. He wasn't as muscular or bull-like as Dave or Simon, but the years in the Army and singlehandedly managing a moorland farm had given him a lean, athletic figure. You could tell, despite his age, that he was far fitter or stronger than I could ever hope to be.

"You're very welcome. Any friend of a Marine is a friend of mine. And from the story Dave's being telling me, you've done a great job of keeping your family alive, and the fact you have without a thought allowed others to join you, tells me you're someone I'm going to like. Tell me straight, did your lad really kill one with a cricket bat?" I nodded.

"Sweet Jesus, the world's gone mad. Now, shall we go inside, meet the rest of your group and have a brew?" I called out to the kids to come with us, and we headed inside. On the way to the door I spoke to Dave.

"How many sentries do we need to sort out?"

"I think we should be ok for the time being. Willie showed me the security he has set up, and we should get plenty of warning of anything approaching."

"What has he got?"

"Trip wires attached to flares at all the weak points, and some cameras set up on an old deer-stalking hide, which apparently have a great field of vision in daylight. He's going to show me when we get inside. His whole place is surrounded by walls or fences, which he assures me are in good condition. This guy knows what he's doing. If he's happy, then I'm happy, but once we're settled in, we can decide on and plan a guard rota. Because no matter how good whatever he has is, there's always the law of Sod, and you can't beat the good old human eyeball mark one as the best warning system there is."

The ground floor of the farmhouse was a large open-plan area with a kitchen area at one end with a huge farmhouse table, and a sitting area centred around an impressive inglenook fireplace at the other. It was a good job it was so large, because twenty-one of us and a baby filled the place to bursting point.

Maud and Jim were busy preparing some snacks for everyone from supplies Jim had fetched from the trailer.

Willie went straight to Louise, who was holding Sarah and asked if he could hold her.

Holding her gently, he pulled faces and tickled her, and soon had her giggling and waving her arms about in excitement. Seeing the activity in the kitchen, he turned to Maud.

"Och, woman, what ye doing in ma kitchen?" Willie growled at her.

Maud looked sharply at him.

"I'm making everyone some food, it's been a long day and we're all hungry. And if you think your gruff Scottish ways are going to intimidate me, think again. Look at you, trying to act tough with a baby in your arms, you big soft nincompoop."

He looked at her and then began laughing, his shoulders shaking so much that Sarah, thinking he was bouncing her up and down again, joined in.

"Ah, you'll do for me, that's what I like, a woman with some fire in her belly. Where have you been all ma life?"

With a sad look in her eye, she replied.

"Until two days ago I was married to the most obnoxious, bullying man you could ever meet. Down to his own selfishness, he's not with us anymore, but I'm not sorry, I don't miss him, and I never will. Since he died, I've made a promise to myself that I will never let what he did to me happen ever again. These people are my family now, and it may seem strange, but the past few days have been amongst the best I can remember having, despite what's going on around us.

I now have a purpose, and I will look after my new family with everything I have. And if anybody gets in the way or tries to interfere with that, they'll have to deal with me first."

Willie had immediately sobered up, listening to her powerful speech. He looked at her with eyes full of admiration and respect.

"Good on you, my dear. I know you meant every word of that. These people are lucky to have you." Becky went up to Maud and gave her a hug.

"You are in ma house now, and I won't have you eating that tinned rubbish. I shot me a deer a few days ago. I was going to butcher it and store the meat, but it's a big'un and there's plenty of meat on it. Have your wee snacks now, because later we'll have a feast."

"I love venison, that's very kind of you, Willie," I said.

"How about the rest of us, once we've had our cup of tea and rested for a while, sort through and repack all the stuff we collected this morning? The back of my car is stacked with guns and stuff, we don't really know what we've got yet. And my car needs some attention, the front wedge is mangled and just about hanging on to the car after what we did this morning. The ride over the moors didn't do it any favours."

"I'll give you a hand," said Willie, "I want to have a good look at what you've done to those vehicles, it could be useful stuff to learn. You're welcome to use my workshop and tools if you want. I've got a small generator if you need power, and plenty of odds and sods of materials you're welcome to have. I'm not going to need half of what I've got."

What a true gent, he had opened his house to us and was offering without condition any supplies we wanted. Seeing a few of us were about to thank him again, Simon interrupted.

"Let's get a move on, folks, the amount of love in this room is making me go all moisty eyed and we can't be having that. Everyone outside now, before I really start crying.

You big bunch of wussies. Jim, you stay and help Maud. I need all the civvies outside, so Dave and I can start to train those who don't know how to use the weapons we have."

A lot of the weapons stacked in my car were still covered in the blood of the original owners. Dave, Simon and Steve gathered us into groups and showed us how to strip and clean them. We were soon doing the basics competently and the stack of cleaned guns was growing.

We had more than enough for everyone to have an assault rifle and pistol each. It was an impressive arsenal.

Once we'd emptied all the magazines we'd collected and counted the full cases, we had quite a few thousand rounds of ammunition for both the rifle and pistols. We didn't have as many shotgun cartridges, but we still had over five hundred of varying weights and shot sizes.

Shawn was in heaven. He kept repeating that in all the drunken zombie survival conversations he and his mates had had, never had it included starting the zompoc with military grade weapons and thousands of rounds of ammo. It was a prepper's dream. Simon brought him down to earth.

"This little pile may look impressive, son, but how many millions of zombies are out there? How much ammo do we have? The answer is not even a drop in the ocean enough. We need to conserve what we have for as long as we can, and keep getting more whenever we can. Once we're down to just having our knives and spears to defend ourselves, we're going to be in the shit. If we have to get that up-close and personal to kill 'em, we're going to start losing people. And there ain't many of us to spare."

Once the magazines were cleaned, Dave showed everyone, including the children, how to load them.

Shawn, Chet and I were reasonably comfortable in handling the guns, so while Simon and Steve went through firing drills, the rest of us, including Willie, turned our attention to the vehicles.

The tractor and trailer had stood up to the abuse they had received very well. We came up with a few modifications which would strengthen and improve what we had already constructed, but the main issue was my Volvo. It had performed brilliantly all day, but had paid the price. Every metal and timber sheet we had surrounded it with was damaged, and the wedge on the front after using to push the tractor, was crushed and looked about to fall off.

Willie and Shawn went off to scavenge what we needed while we removed what was beyond repair. They came back with his tractor towing a trailer full of timber and metal.

"Let me get dinner started," Willie said, "and then I'll be straight back, boys and girls. It's going to be a long night sorting that mess out, but with what we've found, we can make it as solid as a tank by morning." Within five minutes he was back.

"I'm banned from my own kitchen. Maud has already butchered the deer, picked veg from my garden and got most of it prepped. She told me not to touch anything with my dirty hands and to get out and not come back until she tells me.

If I wasn't too old, I think I could fall in love with that woman!"

We rotated a guard from a high point nearby that Willie told us about. It gave an excellent all-round observation point, and everyone spent the next few hours until dusk began to fall, either working on the vehicles or training and familiarising themselves with the weapons.

Exhausted and starving, we were glad when Maud called us all in for dinner.

CHAPTER SIX

The food prepared by Maud and Jim smelt delicious. A separate table had been set up for the children to eat at, and Sarah was asleep in a log basket lined with towels. The scene could have been taken from a family Christmas where far too many people crammed around tables to celebrate.

It was the first time my children had tasted venison, and I was a little apprehensive about whether they would like it, but I needn't have worried. They all wolfed it down and held out their plates when asked if they wanted seconds.

Not long after dinner, the children could hardly keep their eyes open. Willie kindly offered us use of the two bedrooms upstairs and the children were all ushered upstairs and forced to clean their teeth before falling fast asleep.

The night was relatively warm, with only a slight chill to remind us that we were high on the moors, so we moved outside to avoid disturbing the children and to have a few drams of whisky that Willie insisted we all share with him.

All the gates to the yard were securely locked and Willie assured us that we would only need to patrol its perimeter. He'd gone to the high ground while we were tidying away the plates, and using low light binoculars, he'd thoroughly checked the surrounding area and announced it completely clear.

It took about ten minutes to walk the perimeter, so it was easily agreed that we should all take a turn. We were all sitting in a circle in his yard, with a single paraffin lamp providing enough light so we could see each other. Once you had walked and checked the perimeter, the person to your right would do the same, and so on.

The whisky was a perfect Isle of Skye single malt and even the non-whisky lovers amongst the group declared it wonderful, and eagerly accepted the refills that Willie continually offered from the crate of bottles he had set in the middle of the circle.

The conversation ebbed and flowed around various subjects, but always inevitably returned to the story of the moment. The zombie apocalypse we were in and how to survive it.

Willie declared our intent to head to Warwick Castle a sound plan, but refused our offer to join us, stating that he had lived up there alone for over twenty years, and he was so far off the beaten track that even walkers found it hard to find him, let alone the walking dead. He had enough supplies to last a long time and enough weapons and ammunition to keep himself safe. We tried to persuade him, but we eventually gave up when he said he would keep searching out survivors who had fled to the moors, and offer them a place to recover, and would tell them to head to Warwick to join us.

He told us about what he had learned from other ham radio users he was in touch with around the world. Most had reported the spread of the outbreak and he'd had to listen to many desperate calls for help from households about to be overrun. In the United States, many Prepping communities had activated their well worked out and practised emergency plans and had headed to what they had considered to be their pre-planned safe areas.

Most reported very few of their members making it, and were preparing to do the best they could to survive. Very few reported that they were safe and secure in their compounds. We had seen the TV shows about these groups that people call extremists, who the media tried to portray as a danger to national security.

They had secure walled compounds and vast supplies of both food and arms. They trained as virtual paramilitary organisations, and had drills and pre-planned procedures to follow, so everyone worked as a team. They reported, as far as they could tell, the complete collapse of the command and control of the nation's armed forces. The virus had spread too far and too quickly, decimating most of the available manpower as they themselves became infected and turned.

Shawn, as a Prepper himself, had a greater understanding of what these groups had and were capable of, and regaled us with a few stories of the amassed resources these groups probably had available. Unlike the military, these guys prepared for the end of the world and knew what to do, and they didn't have to wait for orders to act which would come too late, but acted immediately at the first sign of any of their pre-prepared scenarios happening.

Simon and Dave explained that a problem we were having was the ammunition the armed forces used. As did all others around the world, the bullets were full metal jacket or ball ammunition. This enabled good penetration, but the bullet was not designed to expand and so cause massive damage to whatever it hit. It just went straight through unless it hit anything solid, such as bone. That was fine on the battlefield, because if you were shot, you were down and out of the fight, but a lot of bullet wounds were survivable with quick medical treatment.

Expanding rounds used for hunting, which were banned for battlefield use under The Hague Convention that dated to the late 1800s, would expand on impact and cause maximum internal damage, and so most likely kill what it hit quickly and therefore humanely.

The zombies could feel no pain, so unless somewhere vital was hit such as the brain or the heart, they just carried on coming, regardless of what damage the bullet had caused.

"Ya need to get yerself to a gun shop, ma boys," said Willie, "The .223 round used in a lot of hunting rifles is the same at the

.556 bullets those SA80s use. They'll have a lot of stopping power and give you a better chance of putting them down. There's one not far from here in Newton Abbot. If someone hasn't beaten ya to it, I'd plan to head there as soon as possible. They won't keep thousands of rounds, but whatever they have will be better than what ya currently have. But they'll keep thousands and thousands of shotgun cartridges which I'm sure you'll find useful."

Dave offered Willie any of the guns we had for him to keep for himself as small recompense for what he'd given to us. He said he had a fair amount of stuff he had gathered over the years and forgotten to tell the authorities about, but he wouldn't mind having one of the SA80s, as it would be a nice addition to his collection. He refused any ammunition, saying he loaded his own and had plenty of components to make a lot of .223 bullets for them.

It was getting late and even though I felt that most of us would prefer to take the illogical but completely understandable option of getting completely pissed on Willie's fine whisky, we needed to plan for tomorrow.

Spreading the map on the ground, we turned the lantern up to illuminate it better. It looked easy on the map. Head to Newton Abbot to raid the gun shop, then get on the A38, which turns into the M5 motorway. It was then a straight run to Bristol to begin the rescue of our friends and family en route to Warwick castle.

Using a city map of Bristol that Willie found, Shawn showed us where he and his mates shared a house. It wasn't far off the M4 motorway and seemed quite straightforward to reach, as long as the roads were not blocked or full of zombies, that was.

"Do you think they'll be there, Shawn? We've seen no survivors, apart from us lot sitting here." I looked at everyone around the circle. "I know we've promised to try and reach all of your family and friends that we can, and we *will* do that. But to be brutally honest, I'm really sorry to say that with the way we know things are, it's going to be a miracle if we find anyone alive. I hope to God they are, but I don't think you should get your hopes up too much."

Shawn leant forward in his seat.

"I know, Tom, and my hopes are not high, but for our own sanity I think we should try. At least we'll know one way or the other. Imagine not trying and therefore not knowing. It would mess with your head too much and probably send you insane. If they *are* dead, we can grieve and get over it and keep trying to survive. We just need to know, that's all." Everyone nodded, quietly lost in their thoughts about their friends and family. Becky turned to Shawn.

"Tell us about your friends, I think we need some cheering up now."

He laughed, "Where do I start? We've lived together for years and have known each other since school. We've all tried either being married or living with girlfriends, but none of it ever worked out. About five years ago we decided that it would be cheaper if we all rented a large house and lived together.

It saved us all a lot of money and saved us from the loneliness of living alone. All our other friends joke we're the oldest students in the world. It works really well, though. We all have our own space, so if any of us has a girlfriend over, we can get some privacy, but there's always someone about to spent time with. We have rules to keep the place as tidy as we can, and we pay for a cleaner to come in twice a week to do all the stuff us boys miss."

I laughed and said out loud, "Wow it sounds great..."

I immediately realised what I'd said and tried to save the situation, much to everyone's amusement, by explaining to Becky that I thought it clearly was not a good thing and people needed to settle down, and provide a stable home to raise their family. She eventually slightly forgave me and told Shawn to continue.

"We got into prepping after many pub 'what if' conversations, and decided that improving our survival skills worked well with our other shared passion. Medieval reenactments. Most weekends during the summer, we pack up our van and head off to the many reenactments that happen all over the country.

"It's great. We set up our medieval authentic camp and stage mock battles with other groups, and display fighting techniques used by foot soldiers and knights. We all love the living history side of what we do, showing the public what equipment we have, from suits of armour and weapons to medieval surgery techniques. But by far the best thing we do is to beat the hell out of each other on the fighting field, or work together to take on other groups. They should be at a week-long reenactment festival not far from Bristol today. I should be there with them, but for some reason I fancied some time on my own, and so I took a few days off work and headed to Cornwall, and the rest you know."

Becky laughed. "Are you telling me I'm going to Bristol to meet my knight in shining armour? Let's get going. Tom, you may get your wish to live the bachelor life sooner than you think."

I let everyone have another laugh at my expense before asking, "Do you think they'll have made it?"

"If they avoided the infection, which from what we know of when it started, they should have. It's a big event and they would have a lot of kit to get ready. We always do the same thing before an event, and spend the day before preparing what we need to take, doing repairs and oiling and cleaning everything to keep it in good condition. It all costs a lot of money, so we don't like to go out to the pub and leave it all out in the house. We always stay at home and have a few beers the night before an event, and then we load the van in the morning and head off. What I don't know is whether they left the house, or if the world had gone to shit before then. But they ain't daft and if they could see what was going on, it wouldn't take them long to realise that the impossible had happened.

"If they'd avoided getting infected and left the house, but ran into trouble, then they would have a van full of swords, battle axes and maces, and the necessary skills to defend themselves."

We were all intrigued by the vision of a group of armour-clad knights fighting through the streets of a modern city.

"How many do you share a house with?" I asked

"There are six of us. If you want, I can tell you about them." We all wanted to hear more, so we told him to carry on.

"Ian Beaver is my best mate and chief trouble maker. He's massive. Six foot seven, and weighs in at twenty stone. He used to play prop in rugby for the county. In reenactments we use him as our main battle tank, no one can stand up to one of his charges. He's like a ten-pin bowling ball getting a strike.

Jamie Clayton, on the other hand, is the opposite. We call him Gimli after the Dwarf from the Lord of the Rings, because of the full-length beard he's grown. He's a stocky, tough-as-nails bloke, who does bear a striking resemblance to Gimli when he wears his helmet. He's not that short, but standing next to Ian, anybody looks like a dwarf.

"Geoff May-Byrd is the Viking. His favourite weapons are his battle axe and his mace, and he and Jamie are in competition over who can grow the longest beard. They had a bet years ago about who could grow the bushiest beard and neither of them will concede to the other, so they're just getting bigger and bigger. Stupid idiots!

"Simon Delves is a fitness instructor. He keeps trying to get us to exercise more, but he's a bloody sadist and after a few group sessions where none of us could walk for a few days afterwards, we chose to ignore him. He hasn't worked out yet that we keep putting extra weight into his rucksack when he goes running. He likes to wear one of those big army rucksacks. His theory is women will think he's training for the SAS or something, and so they'll chase him down the road, begging him to take them to bed. "He can't understand why it hasn't worked yet. We know; it's because he's always bright red, looking on his last legs and about to collapse. Hardly the hunk of love he thinks he looks like.

When he gets back, he thinks we're being good mates by helping him out of his rucksack and putting it in the cupboard, but we're just taking the weights out before he notices. We're running a book on how much we can load him up before he notices.

"Dave Ford is our resident Casanova; or so he thinks. His grand total of long term girlfriends in the past five years is exactly nil. His problem is he thinks every girl who even breathes in his direction fancies him. He can't understand that while he's great at talking to them, and they all chat to him and hug him when they see him, if they know him, still they all deflect his questions when he asks them out."

Shawn started laughing.

"It hasn't helped that every girl in the local area thinks he's gay. I'm not saying how they know, but for some reason they all believe he's just come out of a long-term relationship. And he, even though he's known he was gay since school, has said he's going to date women to get back at his old boyfriend, who he can't get over, and is still deeply in love with."

Louise laughed, "Why are men so horrible to each other? You're meant to be friends, and look out and care for each other, but you just spend time trying to make each other miserable. I just don't get it."

Jim, still chuckling after what Shawn had said, replied, "I kept trying to explain it to an old girlfriend, but she never understood it either. If we like a bloke, we show it by continually taking the piss out of him and trying to trick him all the time. If we don't like him, we just ignore him. He's not worth a second of consideration."

"And for centuries men thought they were far superior to women,'" said Becky indignantly. "In my experience, no man has ever grown up beyond the age of twelve. They all think they have, but stick a few of them in a room together without supervision and just see what happens."

Shawn had gone quiet, staring into the darkness, the light from the lamp reflecting tears that were welling up in his eyes.

Wiping a tear away, he gruffly said, "Anyway, they're my best mates, my brothers. They're closer to me than any member of my family will ever be. I just hope they've made it, that's all I ask." Looking embarrassed at his display of emotions, he stood up and walked out of the circle of light cast by the lantern. Louise stood and followed him. Becky, seeing the men raising their eyebrows and the beginnings of smirks forming on their faces, spoke harshly.

"That's it! Case proved. If any one of you is thinking what I know you're thinking, just stop it. I would say grow up, but that's clearly impossible. He's worried about his friends and Louise wants to check he's okay. THAT'S ALL. She is a woman who cares. Anyway, I for one, really hope they *have* made it, they sound really interesting and I'd like to meet them."

CHAPTER SEVEN

Several Days Earlier

"Clayton, get a bloody move on! We're bloody going to be late and miss the best camping spot. You know we like to be at the back of the field. Whose bloody idea was it to have the whisky last night?"

Jamie, walking out of the house and locking the door, shouted back.

"Beaver, you wouldn't let us go to bed until we'd finished the bottle, so my delicate state and general tardiness can only be blamed on your big, ugly, fat face. You're beyond help, but some of us need to finish our beauty routine before we meet our adoring public. So shut up, and get that bag you've forgotten to load that's sitting on the kerb, in the van and we'll be off."

With more banter and general chat, the five friends settled themselves into the van and set off.

Simon yawned and looked at his watch. "Five bloody thirty in the morning, why do we keep doing this? I could be in bed enjoying the hangover that's all Beaver's fault."

Geoff, who was driving and was cheerfully unaffected by last night's session, replied, "Come on, girls. It'll take about half an hour to get there, then a few hours to set up and I'll cook us all a big fry-up before the punters turn up. You'll be as right as rain by lunch time."

Ten minutes later they were out of the city, and on their way to the grounds of an English Heritage property that was holding its annual medieval festival, as part of its summer program to keep pulling in the crowds.

"Great, the roads are nice and quiet, it won't take long."

Rounding a corner on the A road, they came across a car that had left the road and smashed into a tree. Steam was pouring from the engine and its lights were still on. Geoff screeched to a halt next to it, which jolted those awake who had been trying to grab an extra few minutes' sleep. Putting his hazard warning lights on, he said to the rest, "Come on, lads, it must have just happened. Dave, call the police and ambulance. Everyone else, out and let's help. Ian, grab the first aid kit."

Rushing to the car, they expected to find the driver still in the seat, injured.

"Where the bloody hell is the driver?"

The door had been ripped off in the crash and lay in the ditch. The car was a mess, blood was smeared over the dash and the windscreen was smashed from when the driver had hit it, but there was no sign of him or her.

Geoff had assumed control. One of the emergency drills they had practised as part of their prepping was that if an emergency situation arose, the first one to issue orders remained in charge until things calmed down and got reassessed. It helped avoid confusion, with everyone trying to take the lead, and subsequently causing potential delays in vital decision making. Geoff had spoken first, so he was in command, and everyone else would follow his instructions.

"They must have been thrown clear; spread out and search."

Five minutes later, everyone met back at the car. No sign of anyone had been found. Dave still had his phone to his ear.

"I can't get through to any emergency service. It's just ringing out until the message comes up saying all operators are busy and to try later."

"At six in the morning?" said Ian. "That's' ridiculous, keep trying, mate."

Another ten minutes of fruitless searching later, Geoff called everyone together.

"There's absolutely no sign of the driver, we can't find any blood trails, so they can't have walked off. We can only assume that another vehicle stopped and took the driver to hospital. There's nothing we can do. I say we should take photos to record it all and keep trying the police to report it. There's nothing more we can do here. It's bloody strange but what else can we do?"

Everyone agreed, and after a few minutes of taking photos with their phones, the group got back into the van and continued their journey. All fully awake now, everyone was excitedly going over what they had just witnessed.

"Watch out," screamed Geoff, and yanked the wheel over hard, just managing to avoid a car heading straight towards them on the wrong side of the road. Ending up on the grass verge, they all turned and watched as the car continued to weave and drive erratically along the road.

Jamie, after shouting obscenities along with everyone else in the van at the disappearing car, said, "What the fuck! That guy must have been pissed. Good driving, mate, you just got out of the way in time."

Geoff needed a few minutes to feel calm enough to carry on driving, and he said, "What the hell else is going to happen today? It ain't started well, and we all know if a day starts shit, it normally goes downhill from there." With a general muttering of consent from the now very excited and alert passengers, they continued their journey.

Upon arrival at the field, apart from commenting on their luck at beating most others there, and so having their pick of the best places to pitch their tents, they were busy setting up camp.

Dave still kept trying to contact the police, but eventually gave up and helped everyone set up. It took them a few hours to pitch the tents and set up the awnings and tables and chairs, getting themselves ready for the next few days. It was only when they were tucking into the bacon and eggs that Geoff had cooked on a skillet over the open fire that they realised hardly any other reen-actors had turned up yet. There were only another three separate groups there.

"Have we got the right day?" Jamie asked, "This place opens to the public in about an hour. It's not going to be much of a show if it's just us and those other guys." Looking around, he continued, "Come to think of it, we haven't seen any English Heritage staff yet, and don't they normally have catering vans and other stuff here? I'll go and get my phone out of the van and try and call the organiser."

It was a general rule that when you were at a reenactment event, you left modern devices such as phones and tablets in the van. Everyone tried hard to be as authentic as possible, and a knight in full medieval armour checking his smart phone for messages was considered bad form. Everyone enjoyed immersing themselves in the period, and a forced separation from their smart phone did the soul good, apparently. After five minutes of trying various numbers, Jamie looked up from his phone.

"This is weird. No one is answering and half the numbers I've tried won't even connect. Come on, let's go and have a word with the other guys over there, they may know more than us."

The other group must have been having the same conversation, because when they saw them walking over, they came over to meet them. They all knew each other vaguely from the odd events they attended together so no introductions were necessary.

They were having the same worries. No one knew anything. Jamie had lagged behind, still flicking through his phone. He had stopped half-way across the field and was staring intently at the screen. Eventually he walked over to everyone in a daze.

"Has anyone checked their phones today?" Everyone shook their heads.

"You're not going to believe the things people are posting all over the place."

"Like what?" we all asked together. He handed his phone over.

"See for yourselves." He passed the phone over, everyone crowding around the small screen. It was a Facebook post. It showed a video of two paramedics attending a man who was lying on the floor of what looked to be a hotel lobby. The man suddenly reared up and bit into the neck of one of the paramedics. In the pandemonium that ensued, the video got blurry and shaky as the phone holder was caught in the rush, trying to get away. Jamie grabbed the phone back.

"And this," he said, after tapping the screen to get another video up and passing it back. The uploaded video this time showed a crowd of people stumbling towards the phone holder. He was commentating that it must be a student event and how great they looked. Another person walked towards them, clapping and showing his appreciation of the effort they had made. The crystal-clear video showed the nearest 'student' fall upon the unfortunate guy and rip his cheek from his face with one bite, the victim's screams distorting the audio playback.

"Bollocks! They're fake," said one of the men from the other group.

"I know, I thought so at first, but there are literally hundreds of videos coming up on the feeds. Twitter is full of it too. It can't all be fake. Look at this one, I know the place. It's outside my mate Chris's favourite pub in Moseley in Birmingham."

Jamie fiddled with his phone for a while and showed the group a video showing a police car that had crashed through the front of a pub. The policeman, who must have been driving the car, was ripping chunks of flesh from a screaming woman, but there was too much noise from screams and the sound of other crashes to hear any meaningful audio. The video stopped when the policeman pushed his hand into the poor woman's stomach and pulled what must have been her intestines out and began to chew them.

"I know that pub. It's the Prince of Wales! There's no way that's faked. It just couldn't be done. I'm telling you, something weird is going on. Look what's happened to us already today; the car crash, the idiot driver, not being able to contact any emergency service, or anybody else, for that matter. I'm freaking out here. I want to say zompoc, but that can't ever happen. Can it?"

There was general agreement of 'don't be stupid' and 'of course it can't' from most of the other group, but Jamie and his friends just exchanged silent glances.

"Let's go and check on the other two groups, they don't seem to have done much setting up," Ian suggested.

As one, they looked across the field to where the other two groups were. They had started to pitch their tents close to each other, but not much effort had gone into setting up so far.

Only a few tents had been partially erected and both camps were surrounded by equipment they had unloaded, but not used yet. No one could be seen, and the camps looked deserted.

A man from the other group spoke up.

"They arrived together. As they drove past, one called out of the window, whining that they were all feeling terrible. Come to think of it, there hasn't been much activity for hours, so maybe they're having a sleep after an early start or something."

Geoff said quietly, "Let's see what's up."

CHAPTER EIGHT

As they all walked across the field, Dave said, "Why am I getting a very bad feeling about this?" The friends slowed down at his words, and more silent looks were exchanged. The others kept walking with purpose until they neared the tents.

A moaning could be heard coming from one of the partially erected tents.

"Hi, is everything ok?" one of them called out. The moaning stopped.

A low guttural growl emanated from the tent. Its sides bulged as someone pressed against it. The tent had not been fully erected, the pegs that usually held it taught had not yet been hammered into the ground, so the sides had a lot more give than they should have. The person inside kept pushing against them until they began to lift, and the resistance the sides were giving lessened the more they rose. A person fell through and fell flat on their face. It was a man, thrashing on the ground as he tried to stand up, all the while groaning and snarling.

A woman from the other group instinctively ran forwards to help. Dave went to help, but Simon grabbed his arm.

"Don't!" was all he said. The man had risen to his knees as the woman reached him. He lunged at her, knocking her over, and her friends all ran forward to help. A scream cut through the air, followed immediately by shouts of, "Get him off her." And then...

"Oh, my God, he's biting her, do something."

The screaming continued above the shouting of all her friends trying desperately to separate them. Another figure, unnoticed by the struggling group trying to help the woman, half staggered, half crawled from the tent.

Shawn's friends stood transfixed, unable to comprehend fully what they were witnessing. They watched as the other person, a woman, crawled towards the struggling crowd. Just as it reached them it fell onto the back of one of them, flattening him, and bit into his neck. It was only when another one staggered from the tent that Dave shouted, "Run!"

The shout snapped them out of it and they all turned and ran back to their camp. Ian, despite his size, outpaced them all.

Back at the camp, they all stood in a nervous group, watching the events across the field. Two more figures had now emerged from another tent and were heading towards the knot of struggling people.

Two of the group had managed to escape the crush of bodies and began to run towards Shawn's friends. As they neared, they were both screaming.

"You've got to help, we can't get them off them. They just keep biting and grabbing everyone close to them."

One of the men was holding his arm. Blood was pouring through his fingers. He didn't look to be in pain, but that was probably due to the adrenaline running through his veins and blocking it out. Geoff stepped forward.

"Let's have a look at your arm, mate, it looks bad."

The man remembered his arm and removed his hand from the wound and stared at it in shock. A chunk of his forearm was missing. The injury was clearly in the shape of a bite mark. Now he was aware how bad the injury was, the pain hit him like a steam train and he fell to his knees, screaming and shouting incoherently for help. Jamie stepped in front of him.

"Nobody touch him. We do not know what we're dealing with. We can't risk getting any of that blood on us." It was a harsh and seemingly heartless decision, but it also carried a lot of sense.

The other unhurt man screamed at them, pleading, "You have to help him. He needs to go to hospital. And what about my friends down there? You must help. What are you, inhuman?" Geoff had walked over to the tent and was holding his chainmail.

"No, we are not," he said calmly, "but we do not know what the hell is happening, or what we're dealing with. I, for one, am not going near any of them without some protection. We've seen what they can do, and I am not putting myself or anyone else, for that matter, at risk for the sake of a hasty and rash choice. The main priority here is our safety. We all need to get our kit on and our weapons out, and then we can help."

Everyone stood staring at him.

"Come on, everyone. They need our help. Get to it!" He threw a first aid kit to the man and told him to bandage his friend's wound, warning him to use the gloves in the kit to protect his hands. The command was issued, and everyone knew to follow without question. They all ran to their individual weapon and armour. Once everyone had their Gambesons on (padded coat worn under mail to help protect from impact and spread the load), they helped each other with their mail. Hauberks (full length mail shirts) are very heavy and help is required to put them on, but the group was experienced and within a short space of time, they were on and buckled up.

"Coifs and greaves, everyone," commanded Geoff.

Once the group had buckled up their leg protectors and put the chain hoods on which protected heads and necks, they then reached for their weapons and the transformation was complete.

They were now a group of medieval knights, the only nonauthentic items worn was their footwear and trousers, which were visible below their padded undercoats and mail.

The weaponry each of them carried was a matter of personal preference. Ian and Jamie preferred the battle-axe. Simon and Dave used the two-handed classic knight's sword, while Geoff hefted a vicious looking mace.

The wounded man had gone silent and lay pale and still, while his friend applied pressure to the wound to try and stop the bleeding. Geoff, who was still in command, told him, "You're doing the right thing. Keep him comfortable. We're going to help your mates. Come on, lads, let's see what we can do."

Everyone was used to carrying the weight of armour. It was not the easiest thing to run in, but long hours of practice gave them the strength needed to start off at a jog across the field.

"If this is a zompoc, what the hell are we going to do?" Simon spoke up as they hurried across the field, "I mean, if we kill someone, where do we stand?"

Beaver laughed, "Idiot! You're questioning the legal implications of using deadly force against an undead zombie who's trying to chew your throat out. That's a new one."

Dave, who was considered the group's legal expert because he had once dated a policewoman, said, "Look, we haven't got a clue what's going on yet. Yes, we all have an idea, and if that *is* the case, then I imagine we have nothing to stop us going into full walking dead mode. But let's find out first, before Simon starts chopping the head off everyone he meets."

It was hard to figure out what was going on at the other camp. A few people were crawling away from the pile of writhing bodies by the tent.

"Don't stop, they're alive. Let's see what's going on at the tent first," Geoff ordered.

The first one they passed crawling away was a woman. She was covered in blood and was in a state of shock. As they passed, she didn't notice them but kept crawling, digging her blood-covered hands into the soft earth of the field for grip, her wide-eyed catatonic stare focused on the ground ahead.

The next one they came to had the lower half of one leg hanging off, dragging the barely attached limb, and pushing himself away with his one good leg. The bloody mangled mess of the other leg was leaving a trail of blood to mark his path. His face, frozen in pain and fear, did not register the passing friends.

The scene of carnage at the tent was straight out of a horror film. These people had once been a group of, if not friends, then people they had known and spent time with at other reenactment events. Their bodies lay covered in blood, each with another person, who they had also known, crouching over the corpses and eating them. The whole area was awash with blood, which had formed pools, small streams of it running from the bodies down the slope as the pools filled.

Dave swore and then promptly threw up. The noise of him throwing up attracted the attention of the ones feeding. Six gore-covered faces stared at the group. If a caption could have been written above the staring faces, it would have said 'FRESH MEAT'. The looks on all the faces were that easy to read, the hunger and evil, inhuman venom clearly showing. They all stood up slowly and faced them.

"There is no way those things are human anymore," said Ian, in a voice a few octaves higher than normal. Geoff summed it up.

"We've witnessed those things, whatever they are, kill and eat people we knew. If I'm not mistaken, they are now heading towards us to try and do the same to us. In answer to Simon's question, I would say that we have a clear case of self defence."

He paused. "I think that gives us the right to go 'weapons free'. If they attack us, we can use whatever means we have to defend ourselves."

Ian, who took the lead in the reenactment fights due to his huge bulk, took over command by shouting, "Form line on me, lads. You know the drill. Protect each other's blind side and keep talking. This is for real, so if need be, don't hesitate. It could get you killed."

From years of practice they knew the drill, and instantly formed a fighting line, everyone knowing their position. The stumbling, gore-covered, growling people, who moments before had been feeding on human flesh, grew close. Everyone held their weapons ready.

"Stop, or we will attack,' Ian shouted at them. No response, they just kept coming. The nearest one closed in on Simon, who also kept shouting for it to stop. He held his sword out straight in front of him. The blood-covered being reached the tip of his sword. It paused as it pressed against its chest. For a few moments it snarled and snapped its teeth. It pushed harder. The tip of the sword broke through the skin, yet still it kept the pressure on, pushing harder. Simon was screaming in fear and anger, telling it to stop.

It gave one final push and the blade pierced its chest fully. It kept on walking with the blade sinking deeper into its chest, the tip now sticking out of its back. Simon took a step backwards as it got closer, its jaws opening and closing as if getting ready to feast on his flesh.

Its chest reached the hilt and it stopped. As it brought its arms up to reach out and grab him, he stumbled and fell over backwards, screaming in terror, the thing on top of him, its jaws inches from his face, its hands grabbing at his armour.

Jamie, who was next to him in the line, swung his axe at its exposed back. The blade bit deeply. The thing gave no sign of pain, but kept trying to reach Simon. Wrenching the blade free, Jamie could see the horrific injury he had caused. Smashed ribs stuck upright from the gaping wound, he had almost cleaved the thing in two and it hadn't even flinched.

"Geoff, use your fucking mace. If I hit it in the head with my axe, I might hit Simon."

Geoff immediately turned, and without hesitation raised his mace and smashed it into the back of its skull. Its head caved in and brain matter splattered everywhere. It stopped moving and its head slumped against Simon's chest, clearly dead.

He said, "That's it, lads, aim for the heads. If we're going to put them down, don't hesitate. DO IT!"

The others were almost upon them. Ian let out a mighty roar and swung his battle axe at the head of the nearest one to him. The powerful stroke took it clean off its shoulders, its body falling as the head rolled away across the field.

Seeing that, the rest took one step forwards and swung their weapons. The heavy weapons swung by strong and experienced hands were deadly, and with expertly aimed hits, the rest of the approaching zombies were quickly stopped.

The four friends stood together, looking in shock at the carnage they had caused. Eventually a muffled voice came from behind them, breaking the silence.

"Can you get this thing off me? I can't see anything. What's going on?"

Turning, they realised they had momentarily forgotten about Simon, who was still trapped under the body Geoff had killed, his heavy armour making it difficult to move enough to get the corpse off himself.

Dave stepped forward and with his foot, rolled the body off his friend and held his arm out to help him stand up.

Dave sniffed, "What's that bloody smell?"

Simon looked sheepish, "What do you think? I've bloody shit myself, that's what that bloody smell is." He looked at everyone, his words just sinking in. "Don't even start, you lot. I was just about to be eaten alive. I couldn't help it. Any of you would have done the same."

Ian, with his eyes twinkling, trying to hold back his laughter, replied,

"Oh yes, we could have, but while you were lying on the floor, trying to hug it to death and squealing like the little girl you are, we killed them all for you." He turned to the rest. "Anybody else feel a shit popping out? Or did you man up and get on with it?"

Knowing there was nothing he could do to stop the continual ribbing he was going to get, he just gave a one-finger salute to his friends and turned to survey the field. The two crawling away had got further up the field. In the distance, by their camp, they could see the man still tending to his friend.

Together they approached the bodies lying by the tent. They were barely recognisable as humans, they were so badly mauled.

"That one is moving," Jamie said, pointing at one. As they approached, they could see its head jerking slightly. You couldn't tell if it had been a man or a woman. Its whole stomach cavity was a gaping hole and what was left of its contents were strewn around it.

"No way that's alive. It must be muscle spasms or something," Simon said, stepping closer.

When he was a few feet away, its head suddenly turned towards him and it started to snarl and snap its jaws, its remaining eye staring at him. Staggering backwards away from the hellish scene, he bumped into Ian.

He sniffed, "You shit yourself again?" Dave bought them back to reality.

"Well, I think we can safely say that we are now officially in the middle of the zompoc we've talked about so many times."

He held up his hands and raised one finger.

"This is what we know so far. Number one. It must have spread last night while we were at home, because we haven't got it." He added another finger.

"Number two. It's not localised. We saw hardly any cars this morning and where is everyone else who should be here? We know that reenactors come here from all over the country and hardly any made it. And some of those who did were infected by whatever has caused this." Another finger. "Number three. They're definitely what we know as zombies. They don't feel pain. Jamie almost chopped that one in half and it kept going. The only way to kill them, as far as we've discovered, is to kill the brain. Classic zombie folklore. And the bites infect. That one over there shouldn't be alive, but somehow it is."

He raised his fourth finger and looked at it for a while.

"No that's it for now. This is it, though, boys. We've talked about it, joked about it, told each other it could never happen. But it has, and we need to get our shit together and work on a plan for us to get through this. Damn, I hope Shawn is okay, though. Trust him not to be here when we need him.

"Right. First, let's check on the others over there. If they've been bitten, it looks likely they're going to turn, so we're going to have to prepare ourselves for that. It's quite remote where we are here, so we should be safe in the short term, but we can't stay here for long. Tents are not going to keep us safe and we need a lot more kit if we're going to stand a chance."

Simon was still looking at the one who had turned. It was still thrashing its head, unable to move anywhere. He walked back up to it and stared at it for a moment.

He raised his sword and said quietly, "Tough break, mate. Rest in peace."

He thrust his sword through its eye socket. It jerked once and fell still forever. He walked back to the others, and everyone was silent, the reality of their situation beginning to sink in. Resting their weapons on their shoulders, they walked somberly back to where the injured reenactors were. They'd only been trying to help, but had signed their death warrant by doing so.

Not knowing how the virus spread, they decided that the safest, though not the kindest, course of action, would be to not treat them directly, but to try to offer what help they could from a short distance away.

Dave went and got surgical gloves and paper face masks for everyone to use. They were a standard part of the prepping kit that was always carried in the van and now seemed a sensible time to use them.

The man who had lost most of his leg was in a poor way. He was almost unconscious from blood loss, and delirious with pain and what appeared to be a fever, which meant that communication with him was impossible.

The woman, however, was more coherent. She was in tremendous pain from the bitemarks on her face and arms, and was complaining about her whole body being wracked with a burning sensation. She naturally didn't understand them not wanting to touch her, but to be fair, there was not a lot she could do about it. Simon handed her bandages and a bottle of water so she could take the painkillers offered her.

The one who had reached the camp with a bite to his arm was faring not much better, despite the treatment he had received from his friend. The painkillers he had had were not nearly enough for what he needed, and he was also complaining about feeling feverish and burning up.

When the uninjured one asked about his friends, a small shake of the head from everyone made him stand up and walk away, his shoulders betraying the tears he was shedding.

"I'd better go and tell him the bad news about the ones still living," Ian said, "He needs to know and prepare for that soon, I think." Ian walked over to him. They could follow the conversation from his actions. He returned five minutes later with the man, a very distraught individual.

"If this is going to happen like you say, and from what we've seen so far, I'm going to have to believe you, I'll do it for my loved ones when the time comes. I owe them that at least."

"Spoken like a true friend and a good man," said Geoff, "But we don't know yet if you've caught it. You've been treating your friend and we don't yet know how this thing spreads. That's why we're wearing masks and gloves."

He handed him a new pair of gloves and a mask.

"If you could put those on, it might help protect us."

His name was Marc and he agreed and put them on immediately, promising to be honest and tell them at the first sign of feeling unwell. Simon, who, after quickly changing his trousers and cleaning himself up, had also been checking on the two other injured people, shouted that he thought the one who had lost most of his leg had died.

Marc stood up from where he was sitting beside the woman, holding her hand and offering her what comfort he could, joined Simon, everyone following. His friend, whose name was Jason, looked dead. He knelt beside him and tried to feel for a pulse. He stood, shaking his head.

"Goodbye, mate. Rest in Valhalla, my friend."

The body jerked. Marc instinctively stepped forward, but Ian grabbed his arm and said simply.

"No!"

They all watched, as over the next few minutes, Jason became no more. He was replaced by a zombie. It tried to stand, but couldn't due to having only one good leg, and it lay on the ground, thrashing and trying to claw its way to its former friend.

"Can someone give me a knife, please?" Dave handed him one he had recently clipped to his belt. Marc stepped forward and without hesitation, grabbed his former friend by the hair and drove the knife deep into his skull through the ear. His eyes brimming with tears, he silently handed the knife back to Dave.

"She's gone now," Simon called out.

The woman also lay still, her body curled into the foetal position, possibly in her last moments returning into the position she had first lain in the womb of her mother. Marc held his hand out and Dave once again passed him the knife.

He knelt beside her, said simply, "Goodbye, Janet, my love," and thrust the knife into her brain, ending any chance of her returning. A voice said quietly from behind the group standing around Marc's friend,

"Dad. Kill me now. Just like you've done for Mom. I can feel my body changing. I'm already dead. Please stop the pain I'm in." DAD! MOM! Everyone looked shocked. They hadn't noticed Marc's son approach. Everyone turned to face him. He stood swaying on his feet, barely able to keep upright. The phrase 'He looked like death warmed up' would have described him perfectly. Marc walked up to him, tears running down his face.

"I can't do that, son, I just can't. Don't ask me, please. I promise if you die, I *will* do it, but don't ask me to do it now, my beautiful son."

Marc was loosely holding Dave's knife in his hand. The boy suddenly stepped forward and grabbing the knife, pushed him away.

Marc was trying to scrabble back to his feet while everyone else stood transfixed. Marc screamed, "Nooooo!"

Without uttering a word, the boy steadied himself and used both hands to hold the knife against his eye. He then just fell forwards flat on his face, and the weight of his body pushed the knife hilt deep through his eye socket and into the brain, killing him instantly. The only sound now was Marc once again sobbing on the ground. Everyone else was too shocked to say or do anything, but stare at each other wide-eyed.

His wife and son! Nobody knew what to say or do. Ian slumped to the ground sobbing, and soon the emotions got to everyone and they all followed suit.

Quite some time later, Dave pulled himself together. He walked slowly over to Marc, who was still sobbing.

"I'm really sorry, mate. I just don't know what to say." Marc looked up through red-rimmed eyes.

"It's okay, mate, thanks. I've just got to deal with it. Give me some time. There's nothing I can do to bring my family or my friends back now, so I've gotta get on with it."

"Take your time, mate, we'll be over at our camp." All the others had got to their feet, and one by one, gathered around the smoldering, smoking remains of the fire. Simon threw a few logs on and poked it to get it burning again. The comfort of staring at an open fire kept the group silently pondering for a while longer.

Ian broke the silence. "What now? We can't stay here. I vote we pack everything up we need to take, leave anything unnecessary here, and head back home. We've got loads more stuff there we could use to help get through this shit. We then think of a secure place to go to and work it out from there."

They all agreed to the plan and busied themselves gathering all the gear they had only just unpacked a few hours earlier. Geoff went to the van and turned the radio on.

"Hey, guys, come and listen to this," he called out. They all joined him, including Marc. The radio station was playing a looped message.

"National emergency message. Please stay in your house. Avoid all contact with anyone. Monitor 1050mz on medium wave for information updates."

Geoff tuned the radio to the medium wave channel and turned the volume up so everyone could hear.

"This is the Emergency Public Broadcast Service for Her Majesty's Government. We have very little information about the current situation, but this is what we know so far. A global virus has broken out. Victims initially develop cold-like symptoms but then develop severe psychosis. In other words, they become extremely violent and irrational. Reports are coming in of people being attacked and bitten, and the death toll is rising.

Please avoid all contact with other members of the public until we can discover more about the situation. Do not travel! Stay where you are. We will continue to provide updates when we can. Monitor this frequency at all times. Until then this message will continue to be repeated."

"I think that confirms it then, lads," muttered Geoff, "We're in the middle of a friggin' Zompoc."

The group of six, five still wearing the armour they had donned earlier, silently stood together in the middle of the sun-drenched field.

CHAPTER NINE

Working efficiently together, the five friends quickly dismantled the tents and gathered their gear together, ready to load the van. Marc had walked away and was sitting next to the bodies of his wife and son.

Eventually he stood up and walked down the field to where his camp had been located, returning a short time later with a shovel.

"I have to bury them," he said sadly, "I can't leave them here to rot in a field. It's not how I want to think of them." Everyone immediately offered to help and went to find a suitable tool to assist.

Marc wanted them to lie together, so the friends set about digging a grave wide enough to accommodate two bodies. The soft earth of the field was easy to dig and soon the six sweating men had excavated a hole large enough for the two to lie side by side. The bodies were handled carefully, to avoid coming into contact with any blood, lifted and wrapped in blankets.

Marc, standing in the bottom of the grave, gently laid the two bodies next to each other and climbed out. The sombre group stood beside him.

"Goodbye, my loves. You will always be in my heart. I will be strong and survive this, so you will live on in my memory. I will fight to protect that memory until I can no more. Then I shall join you."

He then silently began filling the grave. Everyone else respectfully waited until the bodies were completely covered and then stepped forward to help.

The act of laying his family to rest, as heartbreaking as it was, brought Marc back from the deep pain and anguish he was feeling. He helped the friends load the van. It was as if he knew he had to contribute.

He had lost his wife and son, he was grieving and would still do for a long time to come, but everyone had to pull their weight if they were going to survive.

The friends insisted that he, for the time being, join their group and accompany them. They explained to him that their rough plan was to drive back to the house they shared in Bristol and collect all the other useful equipment they had there. Then, depending on what they found, they would find and secure a good location.

Marc agreed. He wasn't in a proper state of mind to think clearly, but he could see the sense in doing so.

"Marc, have you got anything you need to get from your camp?" Geoff asked him. He looked thoughtful for a while, staring across the field to where he had set up camp with his friends and family, before turning towards the group. He stood a little straighter and a determined look came onto his eyes.

"I'm going to need to get my weapons first. I also think the pikes we use will make great zombie killers." He looked at the group.

"I think I need to get some better armour, though. All we wear is chest plates, helmets and greaves, and I'm going to want to wear more than that." Geoff pondered for a moment.

"Pikes will make the perfect longer distance weapon. How many have you got? If we work out some new tactics, I think they'll be a great addition. Oh, and don't worry about the armour. We have enough spares to cobble something together for you." He waved his hand towards Marc's camp and the other one close to it.

"I think we should take what we can from your camp and the camp the others had, though. If the shit has hit the fan like we think it has, we're going to need as many spare weapons as we can get our hands on.

Let's finish getting all this loaded and then we'll go and get your kit and whatever else we can."

Working together with a practised routine, the van was soon packed and after a final check around, Geoff drove the van down the slope to Marc's camp while the other walked.

Marc stayed behind for a few minutes to say a final farewell to his family before joining the group, who were waiting for him to arrive, respectfully not wanting to begin rootling through his possessions before he got there. It was soon apparent from the amount of useful kit they could gather from Marc's camp alone, that it would not fit into their van. The decision to use Marc's van, which was similar to the one they had, was an easy one to make.

Everyone apart from Marc was still wearing the armour they had donned earlier. The hot sun beating down and the heavy weight they were carrying made them sweat profusely and slowed down the process, but eventually everything that was deemed useful was piled into the back of Marc's van.

Jamie called a rest break and the rest of the group all slumped to the ground, most likely grateful that someone had called out what they were all thinking, but not wanting to be the first to break and ask for it. Marc passed around bottles of water, which they all drank deeply from.

Jamie started a conversation about tactics they should use in the future, if and most likely when, they faced more zombies. They were all on a subject they had experience and knowledge of, so everyone had an opinion and the conversation took off.

The main consensus was that from the little experience they'd gained from the one brief battle they'd just fought, was that their tactics had been sound. Shields would be useful to hold the zombies back if the numbers got too many, and they would help protect them.

The pikes that Marc had would give them the means to kill from a greater distance, which everyone agreed would be a better and safer option.

From modern times, when small numbers of police using riot shields have held protestors at bay, to battlefields across the millennia, a small number of well trained, well drilled and suitably armed people have been able to stop, fight and defeat far greater numbers than should be possible.

History books are full of accounts of British red-coats forming squares and turning the tides of battle as the enemy fruitlessly washed against these isolated outposts, like waves against a breakwater, wasting their strength, unable to break through. Further back in time, Roman legions fought and defeated countless numerically superior foes through their formidable training and tactics gained from fighting their enemies over the centuries.

The one problem the group of friends knew they had, was that there were only six of them, so there was a limit to how many zombies they could face, no matter how good their tactics and discipline were, before they would be overrun.

Ian had taken a small whetstone out of a pouch on his belt and was running it along the face of his huge battle-axe. Lost in the moment, he was humming to himself. This reminded the rest that even though they constantly kept their weapons in good condition through regular cleaning and oiling, for safety the edges were kept deliberately dulled and not razor sharp.

Noticing the others looking at him, he said simply, "'Bout time we got proper edges on them, boys. We ain't going to be fighting mock battles from now on. It must have been a lucky strike when I took that bloke's head off, because this thing wouldn't even cut butter at the moment."

Everyone else reached for their whetstones or went to the van to fetch one. For the next ten minutes the only sound was the smooth ringing rasp of stone against metal.

An "Oh, shit!" from Simon made them all look up. "I thought you said we were safe here." He pointed towards the entrance to the field. A horde of shambling beings could be seen coming down the lane that led from the main road.

"They're following someone, that's why," Geoff replied.

Looking closer they could see what appeared to be a man leading the group. He was exhausted, stumbling along on legs that were barely holding him upright. He noticed the group, who had risen to their feet and were staring at him approaching, and encouraged at the sight, he began waving his arms and quickened his pace, his faint shouts reaching them across the distance.

Marc broke the silence, standing there surrounded by his armour.

"Can someone help me kit up, please? I assume we're going to help him?"

That galvanized them all into action. Within a minute Marc had his breastplate, greaves and helmet on. With a short sword attached to a belt around his waist, he hefted his pike over his shoulder. Jamie had collected shields from the van and handed them out.

"On me, boys," commanded Ian, "Let's keep tight and stay focused. There are over twenty of them following that bloke, so that's more than three each. Watch each other's back as before, and we'll be fine."

With a 'Let's go!' the six warriors broke into a jog and made their way towards the entrance gate. When they reached the gate, a single command of 'Stop!' from Ian bought the group to a halt.

The man was twenty yards away and had gained ground on the zombies, who had fallen a further thirty yards behind him. At the sight of six men, dressed in full armour and brandishing vicious looking weapons he stopped in his tracks, unsure of and disbelieving what he was seeing. He stood there, not sure what to do next until Dave bellowed,

"It's okay, mate, keep coming, they're almost on you."

He looked behind him at the approaching zombies and then stared again at the medieval apparition that stood in front of him. He looked to either side as if to find another escape route, and

seeing none. He stood for a few more seconds as if he was unde-
cided whether to trust what he was seeing, before running the
final yards towards the knights.

Simon stepped back to let him through the wall of shields
they'd formed between the gate posts. The man collapsed to his
knees on the floor, staring at the group.

"It's okay, mate," said Simon, "you're safe now, we'll be with
you in a minute, we're just going to deal with your fans first." Ian
took command again.

"These gates are where we stand. Our flanks are protected.
This is our Thermopylae! They shall not pass." Jamie laughed,
"Bloody hell, we have Gerard Butler leading us, pretending to be
Gandalf. We're in deep shit now."

"I'm far too good looking to be Gerard, you idiot." He paused
and said in a sotto voice, "And actually, I thought that was one of
the most inspirational war speeches ever given. I expect an award
later."

Everyone else laughed, including Marc, who was caught up in
the moment as much as the rest of them.

"What the hell are you guys like? We're facing a mass of
zombies and you can still prat about. You're all absolutely bonkers."

Dave replied, banging his sword against his shield, "We're going to have to be bonkers if we're going to survive this." And raising his voice, he kept chanting,

"They shall not pass. They shall not pass..." Soon everyone
else joined in, their war cries spurring them on, raising them up
so their minds could prepare to fight the mass of zombies shambling towards them.

The noise they were making made them the sole attraction for the crowd before them. Their pace seemed to pick up as they could see their next meal in front of them. Twenty yards, fifteen yards, ten yards. The chanting petered out and the friends gripped their weapons and shields tighter. Marc had positioned himself in the centre of the group, facing sideways with his pike held straight in front of him in the classic pikeman's stance. The first one was a man in a business suit who must have turned without being bitten, as he had no visible injuries. When he got within range, Marc thrust his pike forwards. The sharpened point on the end of the heavy hardwood pole impaled the zombie through the forehead, stopping when it reached the axe-like blade that was attached to the end of the spike. The zombie stopped dead. Literally! Its arms dropped to its side and its legs buckled, and the only thing holding it up was the spike impaling its forehead.

Marc, straining against the added weight, grunted and yanked the pike back. The zombie collapsed to the ground.

"Again," screamed Jamie. The pike was thrust again. Marc's aim was not as good this time and he impaled what had probably only yesterday been a young woman through the shoulder. It gave no sign of being injured and it pushed and clawed against the wooden shaft of the pike that was stopping it from reaching its next meal. Marc, straining against the weight, held it back.

This caused the ones behind to stack up, unable to even work out that the simplest way to get around the sudden obstruction would be to step around the one in front. Marc yanked the pike back, pulling the spike from the former woman's shoulder. Suddenly released from what was stopping it going forward, it staggered and fell on its face, which caused the ones behind to trip over her body in their urge to reach the group.

"Brilliant. Well done, mate," said Dave, sword held ready, shield held high. "That's broken their line, we're not facing a solid block of them now."

As the zombies at the edges got within striking range, Ian and Simon struck out with their axe and sword. Ian, needing the room to swing his heavy axe one-handed, held his shield to his side, stepped one pace forward and swung the axe in a downwards motion straight through the top of the head of the one nearest to him, splitting its skull in half. As it fell, he yanked the blade free, and raising his shield, stepped back into the line. It was an impressive feat of strength even for one of Ian's size.

Simon was holding his shield across his left side and was swinging at the head and neck of the one nearest to him. The sword was heavy and swung with power, but it took a few blows for the skull to be damaged enough to reach and destroy the brain. The horde was now pressed up against the shield wall, the fences either side of the gates funnelling them together. Everyone was swinging their weapons at the faces nearest to them. Marc, protected by the shields either side of him, held his pike with two hands, thrusting it at any head within range. The pile of bodies on the ground grew, the ones behind stepping over them, pushing against the shield wall.

"On three, push them back," Jamie screamed. This was a move they practised and performed when doing reenactments, so everyone knew the drill and prepared themselves, lowering their weapons and overlapping their shields in one slick move.

"One, two, PUSH!" shouted Jamie, and as one, they put their shoulders to their shields and gave a mighty push forward. Marc knew the drill too, but not having a shield, he dropped his pike behind him and spread his arms across the backs of the ones nearest to him to add weight to the shove.

It worked, the front row of zombies, already unstable, standing on the bodies of the fallen ones, fell back into the ones behind. The force of the push knocked most over like dominoes.

The group had taken one step forward due to the momentum of the push and found themselves stepping on the ones they had felled first. Simon noticed some of the bodies still twitching.

"Step back," he shouted, "some are still alive."

As if standing on hot coals, as one, they all leaped in the air and jumped backwards. Looking down, a few bodies were still moving, trying to free themselves from the others lying over them.

"Close one, well spotted, mate," Dave panted, and stabbed his sword through the head of a zombie that was snarling and snapping its teeth a few inches from his right foot. Ian took command.

"Boys, we've got a few seconds till they're on us again. Kill the ones on the floor and form line. We got about half of them that time. One more go and we'll finish them off." Axes, mace and swords swung and stabbed into any exposed head in the pile in front until Ian shouted the command.

"Form line." The disciplined and well-drilled friends immediately formed a shield wall and prepared to kill again.

Marc killed three more before they were back within striking range. The kills were easier this time, the zombies had thinned so there was more separation between them, allowing for better aimed and stronger swings of their weapons. In no time at all, there were no more facing them, just a pile of corpses lying on the floor. Some were still twitching, so with no hesitation this time, weapons were swung until they were satisfied they posed no more threat to them.

The fight had lasted no more than a few minutes, but everyone was sweating and panting from the exertion. Stepping away from the corpses, they dropped their shields and weapons and quietly bending over, hands on knees, they got their breath back.

"Who the hell are you guys?" a voice asked, "And could somebody tell me what is going on?" They all looked up. In the heat of the moment they'd forgotten all about the man who the zombies had been chasing.

He stood there facing them. He was dressed in working gear, wearing work boots and a hi-viz vest. He had recovered slightly from his exertions, but still had a sheen of sweat on him and he looked terrified. They thought that if they said 'boo' he would turn and run another mile.

"Oh, hi," said Dave, "Are you okay? How long have they been chasing you? You looked to be on your last legs there. I bet you were glad to see us when you did." He shook his head.

"I'm sorry, but who the HELL are you and what is going on?" He pointed in the direction of the bodies lying piled before the gate.

"All I know is I came across a pile-up on the M4. It was a complete mess. I got out to help, and it must have only just happened, because no emergency services were there. Then I saw those things attacking and eating others. Another guy and myself tried to intervene but he got attacked." He paused, reliving it. "I barely got away myself. A few started following me and I've been running ever since, I just couldn't shake them. More kept joining them. I wasn't sure how much longer I could keep going when I saw you lot." He stopped again and held his hands up. "Just tell me why the hell you're dressed like that, can you?" Geoff had just opened his mouth to reply when Marc shouted.

"I think we've got more coming." Everyone turned.

A few staggering figures could be seen in the distance, coming down the lane, following the same route the others had.

"The good news is there doesn't seem as many as before," said Simon, returning from the van with an armful of water bottles. He handed them out.

"Let's rehydrate and get ready again."

"Rehydrate!" scoffed Jamie. "Bloody fitness instructors. Next you'll be telling us 'Today's pain is tomorrows muscle,' or whatever bollocks you keep spouting to whoever is stupid enough to give you money." Marc laughed as he bent to pick up his pike. "There you go again." Ian took command again.

"Everyone check each other's gear. Make sure everything is done up right. Come on, lads, the gate worked last time for us, it will again." The new arrival walked closer.

"I still haven't got a clue what's going on, but you guys saved my life just now. Is there anything I can do to help?"

"Good man," said Ian. "We could always use someone to watch our backs." He pointed up the slope to where the vans were parked. "If you look in the back of the blue van, there's a pile of weapons inside. Pick what you want and then come back here. If you could watch our backs and let us know if we're in any danger, that would be great." Ian turned to walk towards the gate, but turned back to face him.

"But remember the only way to kill them is to hit the brain." They formed the shield wall at the gates again and waited for the zombies to appear around the corner.

"Here they come," muttered Jamie, "Come on, lads, once more."

"Come on, let's get their attention again," Ian shouted, and banged his axe against his shield. He'd just got through the first half of 'They shall not pass' when the words died on his lips. Simon issued a strangled cry, "Oh, sweet Jesus, no, please no." Around ten children, who looked to age from five or so to teenagers, had rounded the corner. They were all zombies, some showing horrific wounds and bite marks and others no sign of injury at all.

"No, no, no!" everyone said in unison.

"What do we do, guys?" asked Ian, quieter this time. "Where have they come from?"

"Probably the same place the others have. They have shorter legs, so shorter strides. They just lagged behind and have caught up now. Shit, what do we do? It's kids, for pity's sake. I just don't know if I can," Jamie replied sadly.

In the silence that followed, the zombie children got closer and closer. The groans and growls they emitted even sounded higher pitched and childlike.

"I'll do it," Marc said quietly. "I've just had to kill my own wife and watch my beautiful son kill himself. If they were my kids, I wouldn't want them to suffer any more. We must do it. It's the right thing to do. They're not children anymore. Their parents wouldn't want them like this. It's going to kill another part of me to do it, but it's what we need to do." With tears running down his face, Ian said,

"He's right. Come on, let's just do this."

The lead zombie used to be a little girl, heartbreakingly dressed in her pyjamas. The only sign of injury was some blood that ran down her face from a cut on the hairline. Everyone paused, appalled by what they were about to do, and unable to bring themselves to strike. The young zombie got closer, the others not far behind. Not one of the guys now didn't have tears streaming down his face.

As the young girl reached out to grab Geoff's shield, he shouted to the heavens.

"Fuck it!" He gave the girl a hard shove with his shield, she stumbled backwards, her arms still trying to reach him, and her face a terrible vision of snarling and snapping teeth. As she fell over, he immediately stepped forward and smashed his Mace into her skull. The small head burst apart. Her body gave a last twitch and lay still, her head a ruined mess, the pink spotted pyjamas the only clue to what she had once been. Someone's little baby girl, loved and pampered by her father, as all girls are. Now she was gone forever.

Geoff broke down completely and fell to his knees, staring at what he had done, his whole body shaking with the emotions he was pouring out.

Seeing he was out the fight, Ian stepped in front of him to protect him from the others, who were only yards away. He suddenly gave a great roar and threw his shield to the floor. Standing still for a moment, his huge battle axe held with both hands, he stepped forward and attacked the nearest zombies with wild powerful swings of his axe. This galvanised the rest into action, and as one, they stepped forward to do what their worst nightmares couldn't conjure up; killing zombie children.

The small bodies stood no chance against heavy weapons swung by arms powered by anger and sorrow. Soon the five other friends stood amongst the carnage they had caused. They stood silently, not able to look each other in the eye, contemplating what they had just had to do. One minute went by, then two.

The prolonged silence was broken by Ian.

"Come on, lads. Let's just get out of here. There's nothing more we can do, let's stick to the plan and get back to our house. The longer we leave it, the worse it's going to get, I imagine."

Five sets of eyes looked at each other and nodded. They turned back towards the gate and walked toward Geoff, who was still kneeling on the floor, staring at the girl he had killed. Jamie knelt beside him and put his hand on his shoulder, saying quietly.

"Come on, mate, you had no choice. You did the bravest thing I've ever seen and struck first. If it hadn't been for you, I don't think any of us would have had the strength to do it." He helped him to his feet and gave him a brotherly hug.

Geoff shook himself down, akin to a dog shaking the water out of his wet fur when emerging from a pond. The act recovered him, shaking off the despair his actions had caused him. He looked towards the pile of bodies, the young ones and the older ones now lying together where they'd been felled.

"We need to move them. That's our only way out and the vans won't get over them." Walking towards them again, he called over his shoulder, "Come on, lads, it won't take long. Take care, though, we've seen too many films where this is when one of us gets bitten, thinking they're all dead."

The new arrival, without saying a word, walked with them, joining them in dragging limp corpses to the side of the road.

Ten minutes later, a lane wide enough to get the vans through had been cleared. Geoff had insisted that he would move the pyjama-clad girl on his own, laying her gently, separately from the other piled corpses. He spent a few minutes gathering wildflowers that were growing along the hedgerow, placing them carefully over her ruined skull, hiding the devastation he had caused.

The group walked back towards the vans.

"What's your story, mate?" Jamie asked the new arrival.

He was called Jon King and was a carpenter who lived in Birmingham. He'd got a contract through a friend of his to help set up a music festival near Bath, and he was on his way there after leaving his home in the early hours of the morning. When he was on the M4 motorway, he came across the pile-up he'd mentioned earlier. He was about the same height as Ian, but stick-thin.

"You ain't from Birmingham with an accent like that," said Ian, standing next to him.

"No, cocker. I'm from Yorkshire, but I moved down about ten years ago when work dried up at home. Been in Moseley ever since, spadge."

His use of colloquial expressions that only Yorkshire folk used, and his broad Yorkshire accent took some understanding, but he was a nice bloke. They explained to him what they thought had happened, through what they had already seen and done, and what the news reports and video feeds they'd found had told them. Then they explained why they were dressed up as medieval knights. He took it all in and in typical blunt northern fashion, agreed that if they were right and the world had gone to shit, then he'd better stick with them for a while until the full picture emerged.

Jamie had heard the bit about him living in Moseley in Birmingham, and they started chatting about what Jamie had picked up from the place during his visits to his mate, Chris. He found and showed Jon the video they'd seen earlier of the police car crashed into the pub in Moseley. It proved that they truly lived in a global village, because Jon said he knew of Jamie's friend Chris, when Jamie had shown him a picture of him on his phone, and they discovered they also had various mutual friends around Moseley.

With nothing else to keep them in the field, they split themselves between the two vans and began the journey to try to reach their home.

They had become seven.

CHAPTER TEN

The first few miles of the journey were uneventful. The road was empty apart from the occasional abandoned car. It looked as if some had either crashed into each other or had run off the road into walls or trees. The spookiest were the cars with their engines still running, stopped on the road, usually with doors left open, indicating the rapid evacuation the occupants had been forced to make.

Geoff, Dave, Jamie and Ian were in the lead van, as they knew the way. Simon had got into Marc's van, along with the latest addition, Jon, in case they got separated. It wasn't easy or by any means comfortable to travel with chain armour on, but taking it off was not an option, as no one knew what they were going to face.

As they neared Bristol, blue flashing lights from a police car could be seen in the distance, heading towards them. The car rapidly drew closer, screeching to a halt and ending broadside in front of them, blocking the road ahead. The police car was in a state, with dents all over it and blood smeared across the bonnet and side panels.

The two policemen inside the car stared at the vans for a few moments before opening their door and stepping warily out. Geoff and Ian opened their doors and stepped out, holding their weapons. As soon as the two policemen saw the two large men step from the van, wearing armour, paper face masks and hefting an axe and a mace, they reached for their batons, and with a snap of their wrists, extended them, screaming for Geoff and Ian to stand still and drop their weapons.

Ian shouted at them, "Don't be fucking stupid, have you seen the zombies out there? I ain't letting go of my weapon for nobody. Now calm down. We ain't going to attack you or anything, we just want to know what's going on.

We've been attacked, we've seen people die and we've had to defend ourselves from those undead bastards twice already today. You're the first signs of any authority we've seen all morning. We couldn't even get an answer from 999 at six this morning." The two policemen stood facing them with their batons still held ready. Ian spoke more calmly this time.

"Come on, put your batons away and tell us what's going on. I think we're the least of your worries today. I've bashed a few zombie heads in today, but as you're clearly alive, you're safe from us."

The two policemen looked at each other, shrugged and lowered their batons. They began to walk up to them, but Geoff held up his hands.

"I'd not get too close, if you don't mind. We don't know how this thing spreads, so if we keep a bit of separation, it could keep us all safe."

"Fair point," said one of them.

"We hoped you might know more about what's going on than us," his partner added, "We've been on shift since last night, our first call was to an assault and burglary out in the middle of the countryside. By the time we'd dealt with it and taken all the statements, we then spent a few hours driving around to see if we could find the bastard who'd done it, because by all accounts, he'd been on foot. No other calls came in, so we spent most of the night on it. It was only when we were heading back to the station at the end of our shift that it hit the fan. We thought it was a riot at first, but when we saw the crowds attacking and eating those trying to escape, we knew something weird was going on.

There was nothing on the radios and we only worked out what was going on from social media on our phones." He glanced at his partner for a nod of confirmation, then carried on.

"What confirmed it for us was when we came across what was left of some of our colleagues from our station. It looked as if they'd tried to set up a roadblock to contain them, using cars and vans. They'd been ripped to shreds. The only possible explanation is that somehow everyone has turned into zombies. We were totally freaked out and kept driving around, dodging the crowds and trying to find backup, or anyone alive for that matter. Eventually our luck ran out and we got surrounded by those things. The only way to escape was to drive straight through them, and we barely got through.

"It's clear there's nothing we can do, and we can't get hold of our families, so we're off to see if they're safe. As far as we can tell, Bristol is swarming with them. If you were planning to head that way, I wouldn't. It'd be a death sentence."

Ian, still with his axe resting on his shoulder, replied.

"Well, it looks as if you know as much as we do. As far as we're concerned, and don't ask us how, we're in the middle of a zombie apocalypse. We've had to fight them in the middle of the countryside, they're everywhere, and on our way back we passed quite a few abandoned or crashed cars. We've been keeping watch, but so far we've only found one other survivor, and he was being chased by a horde of them, so we had to kill them all, including a load of children, which was awful but necessary to do. "We knew Bristol might be teeming with them, so thanks for confirming that, but we're still going to try and reach our house. It's full of stuff we're going to need if we're going to survive this, and it's near the outskirts, so hopefully we should make it."

All the others had got out of both vans by now, and they stood alongside Ian and Geoff. The Six armour-clad knights and one man wearing workwear and a hi-viz jacket looked a formidable and strange group, particularly since Jon was still holding a short-handled axe.

"I'm sorry, but who the hell are you guys and why on earth are you dressed like that?" one of the policemen asked.

"Don't worry, mate, I asked the very same question myself not long ago. I'll give you the short version," Jon replied.

He spent the next few minutes telling them his story and how everyone else with him was dressed as a knight. They asked a few more questions about fighting the zombies, and the best way to kill them, as they hadn't fought any hand-to-hand yet. They'd only used their car as a weapon so far, but they could see from what they'd just been told that it was only a matter of time before they would have to.

Both soon understood all the basics of zombie killing. They wanted to leave, because they were worried sick about their families and needed to get there as soon as possible. They both lived in a village not far from where they were now.

"Would you like us to come along with you, just in case? Your batons aren't much use against them, I expect," asked Ian.

Both the police officers could see the obvious sense in having a gang of heavily armed knights joining them as protection and quickly agreed.

No one had a problem with helping the two out, so they heaved themselves back into the vans, struggling against the weight they were carrying.

The village they were heading to was a few miles down a lane back the way they had just come, so while the two walked back to their police car, Geoff and Marc turned their vans around and waited for them to pull past so they could follow them.

Winding down a narrow lane, the spire of a church was visible evidence in the distance that they were approaching the village. It was quiet as they stopped behind the police car outside a pretty cottage on the edge of the village.

Without waiting for the rest, one of the officers jumped out of the car and ran into the house, calling out the names of his wife and children.

Everyone else quickly grabbed their weapons and followed him. They found him running through the downstairs rooms calling for his family.

"They aren't down here they must be upstairs," he shouted excitedly.

Ian was standing on the bottom step when they all heard multiple groans and bangs coming from a room upstairs. He tried to push past Ian, but couldn't get past.

"Move!" he shouted excitedly, "I can hear them, they're okay."

To everyone else, even his partner, the noise they could hear only meant one thing. But the husband and father was deaf to the obvious, his mind not wanting to accept the possibility that the worst had happened.

Ian stopped on the stairs and slowly turned around to face the man, who was trying without success to get past him.

"Why don't you wait here while I go and check on them?" he said kindly.

"No, I need to see them, they must be going out of their minds with worry by now."

The bangs and groans got louder, the raised voices getting their attention.

The man's face changed as his brain began to process what might have happened to his family.

The other police officer walked up to his friend and partner and put a hand on his shoulder.

"Come on, Bob, why don't we wait here and let the big man go and have a look, shall we? If they're okay, they'll be down in a few seconds."

He nodded silently, his eyes brimming with tears as they both stood aside and watched the bizarre sight of six heavily armed knights carrying shields and weapons walk silently up his staircase.

Once on the landing, it was easy to spot the right door. It was rattling on its frame as the thumps and bangs got more agitated, the closer they got. It was as if what was behind could sense their presence.

Ian turned to everyone.

"Right, shields up and form a semi-circle around the door. I'll open it and step back. Don't hesitate." It took a few moments for them to get into formation on the small landing area but soon they were in position. Ian tried the door handle.

"It's unlocked and it opens in. I'll give it a hard shove to clear what's behind out of the way, and then we'll see what happens." Everyone nodded and braced themselves.

Ian slowly turned the handle until the door unlatched, and leaning back for a moment, he thrust his entire armour-clad weight against the door. It burst open and bodies could be heard being thrown across the room. There was a crash and the sound of breaking glass.

The shock of the assault on them quietened the groans for a few seconds. The only sound was the awkward scrambling of un-coordinated bodies trying to stand. More sounds of breaking glass and smashed china came through the door as whatever was in the room bumped against furniture and knocked contents flying.

The groans and rasping sounds began again and got closer, as whatever was inside aimed for the open door. They had been try-ing to get through the door and now the way was open.

"Steady, lads," Ian said softly. "It sounds like there are only a few of them, but remember it's probably the wife and kids of the man downstairs. Let's try and do this as humanely as possible."

What had once been a woman and a little girl appeared in the open doorway. They stood staring at the wall of shields facing them, as if uncertain which target was the easiest to go for.

"Jamie, get your knife out," Ian continued, "Let's try and kill them as cleanly as possible. The poor bloke downstairs will want to see them, and if we hack their heads off, it won't make his last memory of them any better, will it?"

Jamie dropped his axe and pulled his knife from his belt. "How do you want to do this, mate?"

"Let's use our shield to pin them against a wall or something, and then stab them through the ear. That should make the least mess, I reckon."

"I know why we're doing this, but let's not do it again," grumbled Dave.

"It sounds too risky. They're just zombies that want to eat us, and I'm not going to put any of us at risk for sentimental reasons."

"I know what you're saying, pal," said Ian, "I agree, but let's do it this time and try and keep some humanity for as long as we can."

The woman zombie started moving forward, her daughter close behind. Ian had also dropped his axe and pulled his knife from his belt. Shield held up, he waited for the woman to reach it, before using it to push her against the doorframe. With his face inches from her snapping teeth, he plunged his knife deep into her skull through the ear. Pulling the shield away, he let her fall to a heap on the floor. Jamie had done the same to the girl. With a tear running down his face, he muttered.

"I am never going to get used to doing that. With adults it sort of seems okay for some reason, but kids for Christ's sake, it's just not fair." Everyone muttered in agreement.

"Come on," said Ian, still in charge, "let's check the rest of the bedrooms and then we can go and give the bad news."

A rear bedroom door was blocked by something behind it, and it took two of them to force it open.

A chest of drawers had been pulled across the door, securing it. The room was empty, but a window that led to a flat roof was open, its curtains flapping in the gentle breeze. Simon went to the window and looked out.

"I'd say at least one of the family made it. How many kids does the man have? Let's go and give him the good news that one of his family might still be alive. It might offer him some small comfort."

As they all walked down the stairs, they could see the two policemen and Jon, still holding his axe, standing outside. The look of anguish on one whose wife and daughter they had just killed did not make the telling any easier. Ian took the lead.

"I'm sorry, mate, but your wife and daughter had turned. They're upstairs, you can go and see them now if you want to."

"What about my son?"

"He's not there. As far as we can work out, he barricaded himself in his bedroom and at some point, climbed out through the window to escape."

He started forward. "I must find him." He cupped his hands around his mouth and shouted, "Josh, Dad's here, where are you?" Dave immediately stepped forward and slapped his hands down.

"Don't be stupid, man. We need to be quiet. Shouting like that could attract every zombie in the village. We'll go and search for him, but we need to be careful, we don't know yet how many there are out there, or how they can track us. They have eyes and ears still, so running around making a bloody great noise will not help your son, will it?"

He looked shocked for a moment, but he nodded and apologised. The other policeman said, "Can we go and check on my family now? Sorry, Bob, but we can come back for Julie and Chloe later, mine may still be alive. If Joshy made it, then there must be others."

"How far away is your house?"

"A few minutes' walk across that field there," he said, pointing to some house roofs they could see rising above a tall hedge, "If we drive there it takes you through the village green, and if there are any of them about, I imagine that will be where they're concentrated."

"Okay, then, that settles it," Ian decided, "Geoff and Marc, lock the vans up, we don't want anyone nicking them as an escape vehicle while our backs are turned. There are nine of us, so we should be able to handle ourselves.

Do you guys want to borrow some weapons? If you do, take what you want from the van before we lock 'em."

"Bob, how about those baseball bats we seized from those kids yesterday? We haven't had chance to hand them in yet. They would be ideal. I'll probably do more harm to myself with a bloody great sword, but a baseball bat I know I can handle. We use them when we play the bad guys in riot training."

"Good idea, Jim," agreed Bob, his voice hardened, raw with grief, "Let's get your family and then I'm going to get revenge on every undead bastard we see until I find my son."

Before locking the van, Simon and Dave helped to quickly kit Jon out in some armour. Even though they offered him other weapons, he chose to keep the short-handled axe, saying as he was a carpenter, he could swing a hammer all day and the axe felt familiar in his hand. He chose a shield and tucked another axe into his belt.

"Come on, everyone, stay together and follow our lead. As you two know, we've fought against the zombies a few times and we're better protected than you. If something happens, you guard our flanks and keep watching our backs. But for God's sake, listen to what we say."

They opened the gate to the field and set off. Jim led them to his back-garden gate. He carefully opened it and checked the garden was clear, then walked quickly to his patio doors and peered inside. His voice a mixture of relief and worry, he said the house looked deserted. Ian told him to stand back and they would lead the way. Slowly opening the door, he stepped inside and moved across the room to let the others in.

"All seems quiet," he whispered, "Follow me and we'll check the rest of the house."

Trying to keep the noise to a minimum, it only took a few minutes to check every room. The front door was wide open and there was a car still parked on the drive, but the house was empty. The group walked out of the front door and gathered on the drive. "Any ideas where they could have gone, Jim?" asked Ian, "It looks as if they left in a hurry and on foot. If you were them, where would you run to? If you had to make a quick decision where the safest place around here was now, where would you go?"

Jim and Bob looked at each other. "The church," they said in unison.

It was the obvious choice. Most old churches, with their high windows and sturdy doors, would make an excellent safe haven.

If you could barricade the doors, you would be secure against any zombie horde for a long time.

Everyone looked towards the spire of the church, which wasn't far away.

James pointed. "Look, there's someone on the steeple." Jim ran into the house and returned with a pair of binoculars, and peered through them at the church.

"It's Dave, who lives next to the pub." He lowered the binoculars.

"Come on, if he's there, others must have made it too." He started off down the drive, but Ian grabbed his arm.

"Wait a moment. If they're inside, they're okay for the time being. Let's not rush in. If they *are* there, it's because it's not safe outside. Blindly charging around the corner could drop us in the shit. Yes, we're going there now, but we need to make sure it's clear first. Jim, lead the way, but take it slow. Okay?"

"No problems," he replied, "It's not far and if we go down the alleyway at the end of the road, we can come through the back of the pub carpark and use the wall for cover."

The nine men carefully followed Jim. It was hard to keep quiet when wearing a full suit of armour, but by walking slowly, the clatter of metal on metal was reduced and soon they were hiding behind a high wall that ran alongside the pub carpark. Bob explained that the church was just across the small village green.

Simon carefully peered around the wall.

"The place is surrounded by them. The only door I can see is the main one, and it's closed."

"That's a good sign, the main door is never closed normally, so someone has locked themselves in," Jim answered.

"I don't fancy our chances against a hundred of them,' said Geoff. "We need to think of another way." He looked at everyone briefly before carrying on. "Come on, guys, we've seen enough Walking Dead episodes, you know what to do." Everyone still looked at him blankly.

"Come on, chaps, we lead them away like the Pied Piper. We have two vans, we use one to draw them away and hey presto, job done."

"Of course, mate," said Ian, "None of us is thinking straight. It's simple and it should work if the zombies behave the way we think they will. All of us back to Bob's house and let's get this done."

When Bob got back to his house, he quietly walked inside to say goodbye to his wife and daughter. He emerged after a few minutes, his red-rimmed eyes looking sad but determined.

"Thanks for that, guys," he said, "Let's do this for my son, and Jim's family could be in there too."

Marc, Simon and Jamie volunteered to go in the decoy van. On a map, Jim showed them if they went to the main road and took the next turning along, they could make their way back to the village another way.

"If we can get them to the main road and then get some distance between us, we should lose them, and they won't follow us back. If that doesn't work, at the least it'll buy us a few hours," suggested Marc.

The plan they came up with between them was for the remaining six to go back and watch from behind the walls, while the three in the van would, after giving them five minutes to get into position, drive the van slowly to the village centre and get the zombies' attention by honking the horn. If the theory they were working on was correct, if they drove slowly away and could keep their attention, all the zombies should dumbly follow the tempting meal they were offering.

With a shake of hands and mutterings of good luck, the two groups separated.

"Right, then," said Marc five minutes later, "They should be in position now. Let's do this."

They now numbered nine.

CHAPTER ELEVEN

"I can hear the van," whispered Dave as the six men crouched behind the wall in the pub carpark. Horn blaring, the van slowly drove into the village square and stopped outside the church gate. All of the zombies crowding around the church slowly turned and started moving towards it.

"It's working," Dave whispered excitedly, "they're moving."

Marc waited until the leading zombies were banging against the rear of the van, before slowly starting to drive off. The noise from the horde grew in excitement at the prospect of the fresh meat they sensed was hiding in the metal box that was making a loud noise. As Marc slowly drove past the wall the others were hiding behind, the group of six barely dared to breath, let alone move, in case they inadvertently distracted the crowd. It took over five minutes before the groans and growls receded into the distance, still following the blaring horn and revving engine of the van.

"Ian," said Dave, "take the lead. Let's not change the system. There could still be a few stragglers left behind." Ian cheerfully replied, "Cheers, matey. Right then, let me have a peek around the corner and then we can be heroes and rescue everyone." He crept to the corner and looked around it.

"Shit! About twenty of them haven't followed the van. They're still hanging around the main door. Are you ready, boys? There are only six of us now and two haven't got any armour for protection."

"Don't worry about us," Bob told him, "we're trained in crowd control, and my lad could be in there. Let's go and do this."

"Okay, follow my lead and watch our flanks, we could easily get surrounded. Don't take chances, because you only get one of those. Jon, this is the first time you've done this, so stay in the centre of the shield wall and do what we do. Geoff and I will take the outer edges to give us room to swing."

Jon raised his shield and rested his hand axe on his shoulder. "No problem, spadge."

The four formed a shield wall and with the two baseball-bat-wielding policemen behind, they stepped out from behind the wall and walked towards the church through the lynch gate in the wall surrounding the cemetery.

The man on the steeple starting shouting and waving as soon as he saw them appear.

"Over here, help us, we're trapped."

Ian muttered, "Bloody idiot, what else does he think we're doing? Well, at least he's keeping the zombies' attention on him." The zombies' attention was still focused on the door and the man shouting from above them.

Walking as stealthily as their armour would allow, they crept up behind the twenty or so zombies.

"On three, boys," Ian whispered.

"One, two, THREE!" Ian swung his axe at the nearest zombie's neck. The swing was so powerful it took the head clean off that one, and ended up wedged in the neck of the one next to it. He kicked it away to free the blade, pushing it back into the others who, after Ian's shout, were starting to turn towards them.

Everyone had killed one with their first strike, Dave's sword and Jon's small axe cutting through skulls and destroying brains, while Geoff's mace had completely caved his opponent's head in. "Take it to them," Ian shouted, "One step forward and the same again." Ian, Jon and Geoff kept swinging their weapons overhead, smashing the tops of heads in, while Dave thrust his heavy sword straight at faces.

"Bob, Jim, watch our flanks. They're spreading out," Ian shouted his warning.

It was an unnecessary warning as they had both seen the mass before them begin to spread out as the four knights pushed deeper into them. Bob's first blow caved the skull in on the one nearest to him. Jim's strike was not as well aimed, although it did fell the zombie.

It tried to get up immediately, though, thrashing out until Jim's second hit, aimed with a huge two-handed overhead swing, hit it full in the face, leaving a mess of blood and bone where its nose used to be, killing it instantly this time.

"Keep going!" bellowed Ian. "Only a few more to go." Everyone was screaming their own war cry as they kept swinging and thrusting their weapons at the thinning crowd until Ian screamed, "Die again, you fucker!" and swung his axe in a huge overhead strike at the last remaining zombie, cleaving its head clean in two. His axe got stuck in the solid wooden church door, its blade buried so deep down into the zombie's head and neck, that it remained standing, impaled on the door with a massive axe where its face should have been.

Even though it had only taken a few minutes, everyone was panting for breath from the exertion and adrenaline rush, as they stood and surveyed the devastation they had caused.

One or two of the corpses on the floor were still twitching, until Dave and Geoff walked amongst them, finishing them off. Ian's axe was stuck so deep into the door it took both him and Jon to work it free.

As they worked at it, the zombie it was pinning was shaken loose and slumped at their feet, spilling mashed brains all over Ian's feet.

Bob and Jim then went to the door and banged on it, shouting the all-clear and telling them to open the doors. Muffled shouts and the noise of things being dragged aside could be heard coming from within.

With a creaking of old, unoiled hinges, the door opened a crack. A face peered out. It was a man wearing a dog collar. Jim walked forward so the man could see him better.

"Vicar, it's Jim and Bob. It's okay now, open the doors and let us in. I need to know if my family are in there."

At the sound of his voice, a woman screamed from inside and could be heard running forward. Jim pushed the door open wider and a woman jumped into his arms, sobbing with joy. After a brief but fierce hug, he asked, "Are Charlie and Bertie okay?"

All she could do was nod as they too ran out of the church and clung to their parents. Bob pushed his way past them into the church, calling his son's name.

"Dad!" Bob heard a young voice shout, and he ran into the church to disappear from view.

The group of four still standing outside began smiling at each other. They'd done what they'd promised and helped to reunite their two new friends with their families, or sadly in Bob's case, only his son. As the emotions of the reunion receded, more people emerged from the church, blinking in the bright sunlight.

Most recoiled in shock at the sight of their former friends and neighbours who now lay mutilated all around them, and stared in open-eyed wonder at the four armour-clad, blood-splattered men who had saved them. Jim, and Bob, still holding his son, Josh's hand, walked over to them. Jim spoke first.

"I can never repay you for what you've done. Thank you so much."

"It's not a problem. If we can't help each other out at a time like this, then there's no hope for us all." Ian paused and looked sadly at Bob, "I'm sorry about your wife and daughter, Bob."

"No, I understand now. There was nothing any of us could have done. Josh has told me what happened, and we'll just have to deal with it. They're not going to come back to us now, but at least I still have my son and I have to be grateful for that." He gave him a hug.

"He was very brave and when he saw what had happened to his Mom and sister, he hid in his room for a while until he de-cided to run to Jim's house for help. It was him that encouraged them to go to the church as the safest place to go, so he saved them all."

Josh was about ten and was staring at the armour-clad men in front of him.

"Are you real knights?" Geoff and Ian laughed.

"Yes, lad, I suppose we are now. We are the new zombie knights."

"Do you have a castle?" Ian and Geoff stopped laughing and stared at the boy.

"A castle?" Ian said ponderingly.

"Now that is a great idea. What could be a better place to head to than a castle? We are knights, after all…Sir Ian, I like the sound of that…"

Geoff interrupted his musing.

"Can we survive the next few days first, mate? There'll be time for your illusions of grandeur later, you idiot." Dave joined them.

"Did I really hear you scream 'Die again you fucker' before you split the last one in two?" Ian looked confused.

"Did I?"

"Yes!" everyone chorused.

"Sorry about that, I guess I got carried away with the moment." Changing the subject rapidly, he asked, "How long do you think the others will be?"

"At the speed they were going, it would take them a good half hour to reach the main road," said Bob.

"The way back is longer, but I suppose they would be travelling faster to get away from *them*, so about an hour, I reckon," answered Jim.

Dave looked at his watch.

"It's already well into the afternoon. I think we should plan to stay around here tonight and head off first thing in the morning. We don't want to fight those things at night, and if we hit any delays, which I strongly suspect we might, we won't make our house before dark."

Ian and Geoff agreed. Jon, who didn't know where they were heading, said he was happy to follow their decisions for now. He continued, waving his arm in the direction of the villagers, "I wonder what these folks plan to do first. They probably haven't got much of a clue after just being locked up in the church for most of the day. Why don't we see if we can help them while we're waiting for the others to return?" They all agreed it was a good idea and called Jim and Bob over to them.

There were fifteen villagers, including Jim and Bob, who had managed to reach the sanctuary of the church. They were all still looking shocked and were standing near the perceived safety of the big church doors, trying to avoid looking at the ghastly remains of their former neighbours lying in heaps around them. Ian took the lead in the conversation.

"I'm not sure what you're planning to do, but looking at the time, we think it will be better if we stay around here for the night. What can we do to help you? What do you think you'll do? Stay together or split up and go your own ways?"

"I was just beginning to think about that myself," Jim said, "We have to look after ourselves now and by leading those things away, you've given us at least a small window to get things sorted. Can you all come with me now while I talk to everyone else? You've got more of an idea what's going on than all of us, so you can answer any questions. Don't worry, though, I know we're under time pressure, so I'll keep it brief." He walked over to the villagers and got their attention.

"Everyone, I'll keep this brief, because we've got a lot to do. Most of you know Bob and me, so you know we're straight talkers. I can't tell you why, but from what I've witnessed and learnt from others, I can confirm that we're in the middle of a zombie apocalypse." He waved his arm behind him.

"These guys saved your lives, not Bob and me. Our paths crossed only a few hours ago and, without hesitation, they volunteered to come and help us find our families." At the mention of family, tears started to pour down Bob's face again.

"I've been lucky; my family were alive. Bob as you know, was not so lucky. All of us here will have lost many relatives and friends today, as we believe this epidemic is not just national, but global. That means that for the foreseeable future, if not forever, we can expect no help from anyone. We're on our own.

Now thanks to our new friends, we have no zombies here, but we don't know if they'll come back or if others will find us. You have choices to make. I imagine some of you will have seen one of the many zombie series on television, so you'll know the basics of what we need to do.

I recommend that we all stay here and work together to get through this. But I will understand if you have loved ones you want to try to get to." He paused.

"You only have a few minutes to decide, because we have a lot to do." He turned towards Ian and his friends. "Right, guys. Am I right in thinking that the church is going to be the best place for us to shelter, and that what we need to do now is to gather up as much food and equipment as we can, and get it secured inside?"

"Yes, spot on. Just make sure everyone grabs some sort of weapon as well. While you're doing that, we'll keep a look-out and try to make the church more secure. We've talked about and planned for this many times, so once you find out who is staying or going, we can make sure you're on the right track."

Jim turned and spoke and asked if everyone had reached a decision.

Four of the villagers had family they wanted to go to and had decided to leave. Two were an elderly couple, who still looked bemused by the whole experience, and they wanted to go to their daughter's house about ten miles away. The other two were tourists who just happened to be driving through the village when they got caught up in the events, and they wanted to get home now they had a chance.

The tourists said a hasty goodbye and quickly jumped into their car, which they had abandoned just outside the pub, and drove away. Jon volunteered to escort the elderly couple back to their house and give them a hand loading up their car with stuff they might need, but not think to take themselves.

That left Jim and his family, Bob and Josh, the Vicar, Dave who they had first seen on the steeple, a middle-aged couple and the young barman from the pub.

They all knew each other, and Jim quickly issued instructions, telling them to go back to their houses and start bringing back all of the food they had in their cupboards. The barman said the pub had a well-stocked store room, so Ian asked Dave to go and give him a hand bringing over what he could.

Geoff went to retrieve the van from outside Bob's house and, then he and Ian checked the security situation at the church. The church itself was very secure. Every door including the few small side ones was made of heavy wood and had locking bars that would make them impenetrable. The windows were over eight feet from the ground, so they would not be a problem.

The church itself was surrounded by a five-foot-high stone wall, but the modern need for vehicular access meant that it had a few wide gaps leading to the graveyard, which if blocked, would make it all a lot safer. The traditional lynch gate on the pedestrian entrance had a gate that could easily be locked shut, so the two friends pondered the best way to block the gaps in the wall.

Using cars was the obvious answer, so they went to check if they could move any of the ones scattered around the village nearby. They found a few close by that could be moved and started to push them to where they would be needed, but they didn't push them fully into place as they wanted to allow the van with Marc, Simon and Jamie in to park close to the church when it got back.

As time moved on, they became increasingly worried about what was taking their friends so long. Ian wanted to take the van to go and look for them, but was persuaded by Dave that splitting up any more would be dangerous, and they had to trust in their friends' ability to take care of themselves.

Ian reluctantly agreed and returned to help carry the armloads of supplies that the rest of the villagers were fervently bringing to the church.

Eventually an engine could be heard in the distance.

"That doesn't sound like a van. Grab your weapons just in case," Geoff commanded. All work stopped, and everyone looked towards the direction the sound was coming from.

A single-decker passenger bus drove slowly into the village centre. It was covered in dents and streaks of blood. An armless and legless torso with its head stuck in the front grill was being dragged along, leaving a train of its entrails stretching back under the bus.

"It's them," shouted Ian when he recognised Jamie sitting in the driving seat, pumping his fist like an overexcited trucker.

Simon and Marc were sitting in the front row of seats, also waving madly. Dave waved and, directed him to head to the roadway that led though the graveyard to the front of the church.

As he pulled up, the doors opened and with a hiss of hydraulics, Jamie shouted, "Tickets, please," with a big grin on his face. He shut the engine off and all three filed out of the bus. They looked exhausted and their chainmail and weapons were streaked with blood and gore.

"What happened to you guys?" Ian asked.

"Don't worry about us for now," Jamie replied, "Who was in the church?"

They were all overjoyed to find out that Josh, Bob's son, had made it and that Jim's family were miraculously all okay. Everyone stopped to listen to their story.

It had taken a long time to lead the zombies to the main road. They were hampered by the fact they kept coming across more of them.

The van wasn't going fast enough to knock them out of the way, and they were forced to keep getting out and dispatching the ones blocking the road. There were a few dicey moments when the zombies who were following got too close, and Jamie and Simon had to run up the road, hacking through the ones in front to allow the van to dart forwards to give them time to get in safely.

Once they reached the main road it was thankfully clear, and they were able to speed up, and soon were out of sight of them. The road that Jim had told them to take was easy to find and they were making good time along it until they came across the bus. The destination signs on the front of the bus informed them it was the X79 and its final destination was Bristol. It was stationary, with its engine still running.

As they approached the bus, the reason why it was there became evident. All the passengers of the bus had turned. The bloody handprints on the windows, and the gore that could be seen splashed around the inside told a story that would never be fully explained, as all the witnesses were now part of the problem they faced.

There was no way past the bus and no way to move it without entering it and facing the terrors within. The occupants of the bus had now noticed the arrival of a fresh meal outside, and had gathered at the front, trying to walk through the large front window, their hands leaving red smears as they pawed ineffectually at the toughened glass.

The group of three quickly came up with a plan. If they opened the door using the emergency handle located just by it, the zombies within would be funnelled through it in single file. If they surrounded it on all three sides, it should be a simple job of killing them one at a time as they staggered off.

Not being able to come up with a better plan, and knowing that time was moving on, the three of them prepared themselves.

Marc positioned himself facing the door with his pike, while Simon and Jamie stood either side with their sword and axe respectively.

Simon yanked the emergency handle and the door hissed slowly open. The movement and noise, as expected, attracted the former passengers and they moved towards it. When the lead one reached the entrance, Marc thrust his pike through its eye socket, ending its short zombie career instantly. As he withdrew the pike, the zombie fell in a heap, creating an obstacle the ones behind struggled to negotiate. A few more thrusts from Marc created a small wall of bodies that made Simon and Jamie's job easier, as the zombies behind fell against it and began to crawl over them.

The exposed necks and heads made easy targets as they appeared and in no time, the way was blocked completely by a wall of mangled and chewed carcasses, all either decapitated by Jamie's and Simon's arcing downward swings, or with their skulls completely smashed in. Realising they had been too efficient, and that about five of them were still trapped in the bus, they had no option but to start dragging corpses out of the way to give them room to try and reach those trapped. With Marc and Simon avoiding the outstretched arms of the ones still within the bus, they kept clearing the way enough for them to start crawling over the grizzly pile. With each swing, Jamie became more proficient in the best place to hit the exposed heads and necks to ensure a first-time kill, and the remainders were easily put down.

The decision for them to take the bus was an easy and logical one to make.

The bus, with its higher ground clearance, heavier weight and more power, made a better vehicle to use than a van. It had plenty of space to house the contents of the van and would also give them the capacity to take more survivors and supplies if they came across them.

The only argument they had when everything of use was transferred across from the van was who was going to drive it. Jamie won the game of rock, paper, scissors they played as the way of picking the driver. They left the macabre pile of intertwined bodies next to an abandoned van with the key still in the ignition. It might confuse anyone who happened to come across it, but they hoped that as the world had turned upside down in the last twenty-four hours, all they would be grateful for was a working van.

The remains of the zombie attached to the front of the bus was the only one they encountered for the rest of the journey. They didn't realise it was stuck in the front grill, thinking they had knocked it down and run over it.

Ian quickly brought them up to date on the revised plan of staying in the village for the night, and he got them to continue helping the remaining villagers gather as much as they could before darkness fell.

They now numbered eighteen.

CHAPTER TWELVE

With the light fading and the all the churchyard entrances either secured shut or blocked with cars, the Vicar dropped the heavy locking bar on the front door and stood aside as pews were stacked against it for good measure. Lit by the flickering light of candles and a few lanterns, the eleven villagers and seven knights slumped exhausted on pews or on the floor.

"What now?" asked Simon, unbuckling his arm and leg protectors and struggling out of his heavy chain Hauberk.

"Well, once I'm out of my kit," Ian replied, "we need to get some food down our necks and plan what we're going to do tomorrow. Whose turn is it to cook? And can someone pass me a can of beer? I'm parched and after the day we've had, I believe we all need a few drinks to calm ourselves down."

Ian's little speech roused everyone, and his friends started to remove their amour while the villagers, probably glad of the chance to take their minds off the reality of their world, began to organise food and who was going to prepare what.

A few camping stoves were lit, and Geoff and the Vicar volunteered to cook. They poured the contents of various tins into a few saucepans and created a delicious smelling concoction.

Before everyone tucked into the meal, the Vicar called for silence and asked everyone to join him in prayer, saying that whatever everyone's beliefs were on the ungodly day they'd just lived through, the only thing a lot of people would have left was their faith. He added that if they could all ask for some guidance, good would always prevail over evil in the end.

Heads remained bowed long after he had finished, as his congregation pondered on his words and thought about their family and friends who he had beseeched God to help.

Simon was usually the first to argue about religion and how he believed that it was another way of controlling the population, and how it had become irrelevant in the modern world they lived in. He, however, said the loudest Amen and kept his head bowed longer than everyone else. Ian couldn't help ribbing him.

"Oi, shitty pants, you're not telling me you've changed from being the group's most ardent atheist?" Simon was quiet for a moment.

"What the Vicar said got me thinking. When we first met them and that one had walked up the length of my sword and knocked me over, you know what?

The first thought that went through my mind was 'God help me.' I know there's the saying 'There are no atheists in fox holes', and I would have laughed at anyone before, but why would my first thought be about something I don't believe exists? It's really got me thinking." He then laughed.

"And before any of you say it, yes, my second thought was 'Oh fuck, I've shit myself.'" The vicar had heard the exchange and he went to sit next to Simon and soon they were engaged in a lively discussion about religion and beliefs while they ate their food.

When the plates had been washed in the small kitchen the church had, the group gathered together, shifting pews around so they could all face each other.

Bob told them that they would all be welcome to stay and join in with them in the fight for survival, but everyone knew the necessity of at least trying to reach their house to gather all the gear and extra reenactment equipment they had stored there.

They did promise, though, that they would return if it was possible, once they had got themselves sorted.

All of what everyone had learnt so far about the zombies was discussed, from the best way to kill them to how they hunted. The tactics they had used so far had proved successful and they used their recent knowledge to try and improve on them.

Marc's pike had proved very effective at longer range killing, and ideas were discussed and agreed on how to utilise them in their formation to the greatest effect. The best idea they came up with following Marc, Simon and Jamie's experience at the bus was that, if they found themselves facing a mass of them, they should form line with everyone wielding a pike. They could then be used to build a wall of corpses to hold them back, and then they could change to their close-quarter weapons to pick them off as they crawled over it.

The group in the church had gathered enough supplies to last them for a number of weeks, but at some point they knew they would need to gather more. Bob and Jim collected together anything they had found to use a weapon. The small pile of knives and garden tools was sifted through, and all the villagers selected which one they preferred. The Vicar chose a hammer, which he tucked into his belt, but he had also taken one of the heavy gold-plated candle stick holders and after a few practice swings, deemed it perfect for performing God's work in ridding the earth of the evil that had descended on it. The surviving villagers were of all ages and abilities, but all seemed determined to make the best of the situation and work together to survive.

For some reason, the fact that a zombie apocalypse had occurred seemed not unexpected. Even the older ones, who were not as up to date on all the recent films and TV shows, seemed to immediately accept the situation.

Even though they were all heartbroken, thinking about their family and friends who probably had succumbed, the main thing to concentrate on was surviving and not becoming hysterical.

Bob and Jim, using their knowledge of Bristol from their escape earlier in the day, helped the friends plan the best route into the city. They had come across many roads that crashes or road blocks had rendered impassable. Their information was not complete, but by at least avoiding known problems, they could hope it would go as smoothly as possible.

The bus would take the lead with four of them in, with the other three following in the van. The hope was that the bus should be able to plough through the zombies if need be, and have the power and weight to push obstructions out of the way if they came across any.

Eventually the exhaustion of the day began to tell on everyone, so after a final toast to lost friends and families, and a prayer from the vicar, candles were blown out and lanterns turned off, and soon the sound of snoring echoed around the hard, stone walls of the church.

Saying the farewells in the morning was more emotional than might have been expected from people who had only met the day before and hardly knew each other. Jim and Bob both had tears in their eyes as they shook hands and waved goodbye, reminding them to return as soon as possible.

Slowly, the bus, with the van following close behind, pulled away from the church and the seven continued their journey towards the unknown horrors of Bristol.

They were back to seven.

CHAPTER THIRTEEN

Passing where they had met Jim and Bob, Jamie, the driver, said, "It seems like a year ago we were last here, but it was just yesterday."

They continued along the main road, weaving around the occasional abandoned vehicle, and Bristol drew closer. It was marked by a smear of dense, black smoke drifting across the horizon. Nearing the city, they started to come across zombies, either on their own or in small groups. All were heading towards the smoke drifting across the distant skyline. If he could, Jamie aimed the bus straight at them and drove over them, the sound of bones splintering and bodies breaking clearly audible in the bus. Some of the broken, bent bodies left in their wake still twitched when the brain was not destroyed.

If a larger group was encountered, Jamie aimed the bus at the largest concentration, using it to kill as many as he could and then the others stepped from the bus and attacked the rest.

This kept working until they kept encountering even larger hordes, the closer they got to the city.

"They're all heading to the city," puzzled Jamie, "The smoke from the fires can be seen for miles in all directions. Maybe that's what's drawing them in."

"Bloody worrying, isn't it?" replied Ian, staring at them out of the window, "If they're all heading where we are, it could get interesting soon."

Rather than trying to kill as many as they could, Jamie started to steer a course around the larger groups, when the head of one they ran over had put a large crack in the window as it smashed against the glass.

It became clear that the main road was channelling the zombies in a single direction, concentrating them and making it harder to steer past them. Using their local knowledge, they decided to veer off it and start using smaller side roads. Encountering fewer zombies, they edged into the city outskirts.

Jamie stopped the bus when they crested a hill that gave a view of most of the city. Geoff pointed out a tower block that was not far from their house.

"The fires don't seem to be in our neighbourhood yet, that's one good thing, at least." Marc pulled the van next to the bus. Jamie opened the door so they could talk.

"This is it then, mates. Almost there. This road joins the route we planned last night soon, so we'll be back on track. If we meet zombies, the roads are going to be too narrow to dodge them. I'll plough straight through them and hope the front windscreen doesn't fall out, but just in case it all goes tits up, everyone get ready for a run." He then got a panicked look on his face.

"Who's got a set of bloody house keys?" He patted his sides as if checking his pockets, which were not there as he was wearing chainmail. Simon pulled at a lanyard that he had around his neck and jangled a bunch of keys.

"Got 'em. I had a thought a while back, and got them out of my rucksack."

"Good one, pal," said Jamie, "We'd have been the dickheads who fought through thousands of zombies and then died on our own front door step when we found we were locked out."

With a shout of "Let's do this!" he closed the door and the little convoy drove on.

The first few streets they went down were eerie and deserted. Not a soul could be seen. House front doors wide open and bags and other possessions scattered along the footpaths and across the road, indicating a quick and rapid departure by the owners. Some of the cars that remained had panels dented and bumpers ripped off, telling a story of the panicked actions of the driver of the car parked in front or behind it.

"Where is everyone?" asked Dave. "This is bloody spooky. It's straight out of a post-apocalyptic movie."

Geoff gave a short laugh. "Not here is all that matters at the moment. If zombie folklore is right, they prefer to form large packs, so my best guess is that somewhere round here is a whole lot of them, probably surrounding some unlucky sods they've got cornered. Just keep going, we're almost there." Rounding a final corner and entering their road, Jamie angrily shouted,

"Dammit! There are a few hanging around our front door. Hang on to something, I have an idea."

He turned the wheel and the bus mounted the pavement and drove straight through the garden hedge of a house two down from theirs. He bounced over lawns and through another hedge and a low wooden fence. Steering to get as close to their house as possible, he smashed through the zombies. They flew through the air and crumpled against the neighbour's brick wall. Satisfied they were no longer a threat, he reversed the bus and brought it to a halt directly outside their front door.

He was grinning smugly to himself as he opened the door of the bus and said,

"Jamie's door-to-door delivery service. Please leave your tips for the driver as you exit, and mind the gap as you step off, folks."

Ian turned to him.

"Do you call that parking? There's at least a six-inch gap you're expecting me to leap across. The problem is how are we going to get in now?" Jamie's grin fell from his face.

"Shit. Simon has the keys."

"Yes, dipstick! And he's in the other van. So, what are you going to do now, driver?" He thought for a moment and swivelled his head to check the surroundings. Marc hadn't followed him across the front lawns and had pulled the van up at the end of the driveway that led from the front door.

"As nobody appreciates my genius, give me a sec and I'll shuffle this thing a bit and then Marc can use the van to block the gap I leave. Will that make you happy, Beaver?"

He opened his window and told Marc the new plan. After a few minutes of shunting backwards and forwards, the bus and the van were parked as close to the door as possible, both vehicles now forming a solid shield surrounding the door to their house.

"Let's get in and get sorted," Jamie said, opening the door, "The sooner we can get loaded up and back out to open countryside, the better."

While they'd been driving along, the friends had drawn up a list of what they wanted to take and the priority in which it should be loaded. Now they had the bus there was no limit to what they could take with them, so the list was long and varied from crossbow bolts and fishing equipment to toilet paper and toothpaste.

Simon stepped from the van and fumbled through the bunch of keys on his lanyard, trying to find the right one. Just as he was about to insert it in the lock, the door opened.

A man in full armour, holding a sword in front of him, stood blocking the doorway.

"Who the fuck are you?" Simon demanded, taking a step back. The man lifted the visor on his helmet.

"Simon, it's Alex... Alexander Kirkley."

"Alex! Bloody hell, mate, what are you doing here?"

"Not too long a story, but do you want to come inside quickly? The noise you've just made will surely attract more of them." Everyone trooped through to the kitchen and stood facing Alex.

The ones who knew Alex shook his hand and Simon introduced him to Marc and Jon.

"This is Alex, he lives near Oxford somewhere. We got to know him at various reenactment events. He's a cracking bloke and fitted right in with us idiots. We keep trying to get him to join our group, but he likes the one he's in, so he doesn't want to let them down. Anyway. He's been here a few times and we've had some classic nights out around Bristol."

There were a few chuckles as hazy memories of those mad alcohol-fuelled nights were remembered.

"Come on then, pal, tell us why you're here. And how the hell did you get in?"

"I was on my way to that event near here yesterday morning. I was coming up from a mate's place on the south coast, so I was making my own way there and meeting my group at the venue. It was weirdly quiet on the drive, but I didn't know what was going on until I came across a crash on the main road. It was horrific, half the people were being eaten by the others.

"I didn't have a clue what was going on and almost shit myself when a few I hadn't noticed began clawing at my car windows. So I panicked, reversed the hell out of there, and took to the side roads. I drove like a lunatic for a few miles until I'd calmed down enough to stop. It was then I turned on the radio and checked out my phone and worked out that the impossible had somehow happened." He paused for a moment to gather himself.

"Not knowing what to do, I just carried on driving. It wasn't until I saw a sign for Bristol that I thought about you guys. Looking at a map, I knew your house wasn't far away, so I worked out a route through the side roads and hoped you were going to be in. Having seen what they could do if they caught you, I put my armour on as a precaution and set out.

"I almost made it all the way, but I came across a blocked road not far from here. Before I could get out of there, a load more came up behind the car, trapping me in. All I could do was get out and run away. I had to fight through a few of them, learning quickly that aiming at their heads was the only way to put them down."

"Bloody hell. And you were on your own too?" Dave said. "Yeah. Well, so I started running, hacking at any that got in my way until I got here and found you weren't. They were still following me, and I knew I couldn't keep getting away from them much longer. I didn't know what the hell to do. I was going to break a window, but then I thought they would just climb in after me. But then it came to me. You hide a spare key!

"Remember that night out we had? It wasn't until Dave buggered off with that girl that we realised he had the only key. We had to use that spare one you keep under the rock by the flower pot, so praying it was still there, I found it and let myself in. The problem was that a lot had followed me, so I found myself trapped.

"I had no option but to stay put, so I secured the house as best as I could and I've just been keeping as quiet as possible. I just hid out in the back room, trying to work out what to do next. Most of the zombies had wandered off by this morning, so my plan to be quiet had worked.

I was still doing that and was having a kip on the sofa, hoping they'd be gone when I woke. I was planning to make my escape if they were. But then while I was noddying, your bus crashing through the front gardens woke me up. How, and why on earth are you driving a bus anyway?"

The friends then told their story, with everyone adding bits others had missed.

Geoff then explained what their plan was and asked Alex if he wanted to, at long last, join their group.

He did have family who he was clearly very worried about, as did everyone else, but he could see the advantages of working together as a group. He agreed to join them after Ian had explained that once they'd found a secure location, their plan was to try and rescue as many family and friends as possible.

They were now eight.

CHAPTER FOURTEEN

"Once we've had this cuppa, can everyone start getting the things as I read them off the list? I want some of it stacked in the front room, so we can put it on top at the end, but the rest can go straight on the bus as you bring it down. If you can put stuff such as sleeping bags, etcetera, together in vague order on the bus, it will make them easier to find later.

"Jon, Alex and Marc, as you don't know where anything is, can you take stuff off the others as they bring it down, please, and keep putting it on the bus? That should speed things up. I think it'll make sense to remove our armour, though. It'll kill us to keep trudging up and down the stairs if we're wearing it."

No one disagreed with Geoff's plan, so as soon as the mugs of tea were drained, and everyone had helped each other out of their armour, they all set to the task with a sense of purpose.

Within an hour, most of the items had been gathered and were either on the bus or stacked in the front room, waiting to be loaded. Everything stopped when Jon, who had been carrying another load out to the bus, ran back shouting.

"Zombies, fucking loads of them at the end of the road."

They all ran out of the front door and into the bus where the high rear window gave a clear view towards where Jon said they were. One hundred yards away at the junction of their road and the next, a solid mass of the undead had gathered.

Dave was about to speak when Ian held his fingers to his lips, indicating to them all to be quiet. He then pointed to the house and walked slowly and quietly back inside, shutting the door when the last one was in. Without any commands, they all began donning their armour again.

Spare items had been found and put aside for both Marc and Jon, and they struggled to put on the unfamiliar items until they were helped by the others.

"What now?" Jon asked, with a tremor in his voice.

"We sit here and have another cup of tea and be as quiet as we can. They may not notice us, and hopefully, they'll move on," said Ian, with a grin and a shrug.

"Dave, your room overlooks the front. Go up there and keep an eye on them. I'll bring your tea up when the water's boiled." He nodded and walked out of the kitchen.

Thirty nervous minutes passed. Dave kept a running commentary going, passed via Simon who had sat on the stairs to pass messages along to avoid shouting. The zombies hadn't moved far, some had wandered off, but a crowd, hundreds strong, still gathered at the end of the road.

Alex put forward the theory that they might have heard them earlier while loading the bus, or followed the noise they'd made driving through the city. He wondered if they'd lost the trail as soon as they'd gone quiet, and now were just waiting until another noise attracted them. A sound idea that no one could disagree with.

Time moved on and still the herd didn't move. To pass the time, Ian got a map out and they discussed where the best place to head would be. After endless options were rejected due to

130

distance, difficulty of securing premises, or just too many undead, the obvious choice was to head back to the church. They knew it was secure, it contained friendly people and it wasn't far away. It would, at the very least, provide an ideal base to give them the time to decide their next move.

Everyone's ears picked up the distant sound of a dog barking. Dave's whispered commentary confirmed it. He reported as soon as the dog started barking that the zombies turned towards the noise and started moving away.

"As soon as they're clear, we'll carry on. Saved by a dog, who would have thought?"

When Dave reported the last zombie had disappeared from view, following the now distant barking of a dog, everyone continued hauling the mass of equipment from the house and onto the bus. They realised that even though they had a lot of survival food stored from their prepping hobby, more would not go amiss. As soon as the bulk of the stuff was on the bus, Ian Jamie and Alex started breaking into the neighbours' houses and taking what they could find.

After kicking the door in of a house which was still locked a few doors down, and discovering the family had turned, but were still inside, they only entered houses where doors were left open, indicating it was empty. Axes and swords soon ended the threat, but so many houses were left unlocked that the risk of entering a locked one was not worthwhile.

Walking out of the door holding two bags, Geoff declared that they'd probably got everything worth having. He asked them all to do a last sweep of their rooms to check for anything missed, and said they might as well get back to the church.

"Can I hear that dog again?" asked Dave. The sound of a dog barking could again be heard. It was coming from a different direction, but appeared to be getting closer.

"There it is!" exclaimed Jon, pointing towards the other end of the street. The dog stood looking in all directions as if unsure of what direction to take. It turned the way it had come and barked again. It was a large brown dog, and although it was too far away to ascertain the breed, it looked to be a Labrador. Ian put his fingers to his mouth and emitted a loud whistle. The dog's ears pricked up at the sound and its head immediately turned in their direction.

It began running towards them as soon as it figured out where the whistle had come from. Squeezing through the gap between the house and the van, it jumped up to Ian, wagging its tail furiously. It was a male chocolate Labrador, and it was huge. Ian crouched down to pet him more and the dog knocked him over, licking his face, his wagging tail and making his whole body shake with happiness.

"I've always wanted a dog," Ian spluttered between licks.

Everyone was smiling at the scene.

"At last, someone who likes you," laughed Geoff, "A big fat lab for a big fat, ugly bastard. You're a perfect match." The dog had distracted them all.

"Shit. The daft bugger has led them straight back here," shouted Alex. The street where the dog had come was filling with zombies. Suddenly serious again, Ian scrambled back to his feet and assessed the situation.

"They'll be on us before we can get the vehicles moved. Grab your weapons, boys, we're going to have to thin them out to get through them. Crossbows, pikes and hand weapons, everyone."

The last items to be loaded on the bus were the weapons. The crossbows they kept in the house as part of their prepping had all been assembled earlier, and every bolt they could find put into quivers, ready for instant use. Instantly organised, everyone grabbed what they needed. Marc handed out the pikes from the back of his van, and then reversed it slightly to create a large enough gap for them to walk through.

Ian, who had issued the first command, was now in charge.

They stood in a loose line outside their house, facing the hundreds of zombies shambling towards them. The dog stuck close to Ian, growling and barking.

Emerging from the protective shield provided by the bus and the van, they had been spotted, and the volume of the groans and wails increased.

"Crossbows ready! Start dropping them." The weight of armour they were encumbered with made the job of cocking and fitting a bolt into a crossbow harder than normal. The five friends, being more used to the equipment, were faster than Jon, Alex and Marc, and soon the first bolts were flying towards their targets.

Wearing a heavy suit of armour made aiming from a standing position difficult, but the zombies were packed close together. The first shots hit, but no head shots were scored, so although the undead staggered from the force of the bolts, they kept coming. By the time the first crossbow was reloaded, the distance was down to thirty yards. Simon was the first to fire and he hit one straight through the eye; it dropped instantly. The ones behind it fell over the cadaver, creating an obstacle which held that part of the horde back. More of them blindly fell over the obstruction in their eagerness to taste human flesh.

The closer they got, the more killing shots were made, causing more blockages. The zombies slowly staggered around them like a sluggish tide around a rock on a beach, and continued on. What had started out as a packed, terrifying horde began to stretch out. Instead of one solid mass, there were now spaces between them.

"One more volley, then grab the pikes. Come on, we can do this," Ian screamed. From eight shots, four more were downed. The others walked on, with the short bolts tipped with coloured flights sticking out of various parts of their corpses. Crossbows were slung across shoulders, and pikes grabbed. It took two hands to wield a shield, so they were kept on the ground, close to hand for when they would be needed.

"Jon, you stand back and keep watch on our flanks and our back, same idea as at the church."

"Gotcha, mate," he replied.

"Raise your pikes!" Ian commanded, "Two paces forward and let's start killing the bastards."

The two paces brought the pikes within range of the pack leaders. Proper pike drill took years to master and apart from Marc, who had been using one for years, the first thrusts didn't kill, but struck the necks, chests or arms of their intended victims. The thrusts didn't kill, but at least it was holding the zombies back, stopping them from getting closer.

Straining and grunting, the men yanked the pikes out of the bodies and thrust again. The pile of corpses started to grow, but the horde was large and the line of attackers small. The zombies began to spill around the sides, threatening to outflank them.

"Step back, watch your sides," Ian grunted though thrusts, "Jon, grab our shields."

Jon turned and threw his pike back towards the house. Picking three shields up at a time, he quickly threw them back too. Then he ran to the sides, bravely hacking at the heads of the zombies outflanking them. The inexorable tide kept coming. Every step back they took added more to the kill count, but they were too few, and the horde too great to stop.

When Jon bellowed, "More coming from behind," they knew they were defeated and the only option was to retreat back into the house.

"Back to the van. Shield wall!" Ian ordered. As soon as the command was issued, everyone disengaged, turned and ran the ten yards back to the van. Pikes were thrown through the gap they had used to exit, shields grabbed and hefted.

They turned to find the zombies were nearly on them. Before Ian could react, the lead one grabbed him and bit down on his arm. Not having had time to draw his weapon, he kept smashing his other mail clad hand at the zombie's head, but he could not dislodge it.

The dog, which had been barking and snapping at anything close to him, leapt up at the zombie, his huge jaws clamping onto its face. The dog's weight dislodged it, knocking it to the floor. With a last snap, the dog ran back between Ian's legs, where he continued barking. Wiping a few teeth away that were sticking out of his armour, he raised his shield to join the end of the shield wall the others had formed.

It was impossible, no matter how many they killed and how high a wall of bodies they formed, hacking and stabbing, destroying brains with every strike, they kept coming, crawling over the wall of undead, their teeth snapping and arms reaching out to claim the next victim.

The sweating, panting, swearing, shield wall was pushed back, inch by inch, blood, gore and brains coating blades, shields and armour.

"Hold them at the gap. Marc, you go first and start the van. As soon as we're through, block the hole."

"Push back on my command," Marc shouted. "I'm pulling back in three, two, one."

At the count of one, they utilised their well-practised pushback manoeuvre. This gave them the few feet of space they needed for Marc to pull back from the shield wall and give them enough time to close ranks again, forming a solid wall of metal-embossed wooden shields once more. Marc slipped through the gap and started the van.

The seven fighting men now found themselves in a semi-circle, the shield wall hard up against the van on one side and the house wall the other. The weight of the undead pushing against them increased as they compressed together, trying to reach them. Arms reached over grabbing at helmets. The shouts and screams of anger were now tinged with an edge of fear, as they ducked and dodged the clawing, searching fingers. Only Jon in the centre of the wall had room to swing his hand axe, the others pressed shoulder to shoulder, unable to gain the room to free their arms and swing.

"Fuck me, lads, we need to get inside now. This isn't fun anymore," shouted Ian. He was stamping on the head of a zombie that had been knocked to the floor and was trying to reach under the shields.

"Jon, you go next." Jon pulled away and darted through the gap. He immediately appeared again, standing on the roof of the van, holding a pike. His angle from up on high made it easier to stab at the heads of the zombies and after a few minutes the pressure on the shield wall was released enough to allow Dave to disengage and retreat through the gap. He too scrambled up onto the roof of the van, and with another pike, started to kill the ones in the crowd nearest to his five friends.

The dead ones all remained upright, held there by the crush of bodies, unable to fall, but also unable to do any more harm. Not having to avoid the arms reaching over his shield, but still using all his strength to hold them back, Ian had the chance to look around and assess the situation. He was closest to the wall, and therefore the gap that led to safety. Simon was at the other end, tight up against the van, with Jamie, Alex and Geoff the middle men.

"Simon, when you can, step back and you three fill the gap. Then you next, Geoff. Then Alex. Jamie, once Alex is through, we'll back through and hold them back until Marc moves the van and closes the gap."

One by one, they backed through the gap until Ian, with Jamie using his shield against his back to hold him up, backed slowly through the gap. The second he was clear, Marc shouted to Dave and Jon to hold on, and he slammed the van forward, crushing six zombies against the wall, blood spraying over the windscreen.

Dave and Jon, who had thrown themselves to the roof of the van at Marc's warning, lowered themselves down and the eight stood in a tight group, wide-eyed, faces streaked with sweat and splashes of blood. They stood there, staring at each other, not believing they had lived through the terror of the last minutes.

"Inside," gasped Ian, "We need to get all this blood and shit off us fast. We don't know if it will infect us or not." Panicked by the thought, they all rushed inside and emptied the cupboards in the kitchen to find spray cleaners and disinfectants to clean themselves up as quickly as possible.

A few minutes and a few rolls of kitchen towels later, they were satisfied that they'd removed the zombie blood from all their exposed skin.

"What now?" asked Simon. "We're stuck in here and all of our kit is out in the bus." Looking through the front window of the house, they were relieved to discover that the van and the bus were still holding the mob back, leaving the small area outside the door clear of the infected.

If they were, as they feared, trapped in the house, they would need to get essential supplies and equipment back from the bus. Geoff retrieved his list from his pocket and quickly ticked off items they would need. Weapons and food came first. The first priority though, was to make sure no zombies could crawl through any gaps or holes around the vehicles. Before going outside, they rushed through the house, dragging chairs, wardrobes and any other items of furniture they could use, near the front door to reinforce their defences.

The raspy groans and growls from the hundreds of zombies forcing themselves against the vehicles was deafening. They knew the men were inside, it was pointless trying to be quiet, so as soon as they opened the door, they ignored the noise and dragged everything outside and filled the gaps under the vehicles, and at other potentially weak points.

Satisfied they had done the best they could, they took what they needed from the bus. The rocking caused by hundreds of bodies pushing against it was disconcerting, but forming a human chain, what they needed was soon unloaded and the friends trooped back into the house.

"That didn't go to plan," Ian said as he sat on one of the few remaining chairs in the kitchen. Jumping up, he said, "Where is that dog? Did you see him get that zombie off me? It was amazing." Dave, who was leaning against the doorframe, said, "You have to see this, he's in the lounge."

The huge dog was fast asleep, lying on his back, legs in the air with his tongue lolling out of his mouth. Sensing he was being watched, he opened his eyes, and with his tail wagging, squirmed to make himself more comfortable, letting out a large and obnoxious fart in the process.

Crying with laughter and gagging from the smell, everyone retreated to the fresher air of the kitchen.

"Ian!" laughed Simon, "that can only be your dog, at last we've found something with a worse arse than Beaver. They're made for each other." Ian, trying to look indignant, replied, "That dog saved my life earlier, and I will not have a bad thing said about it. No matter what any of you say, he is staying. He saved us all by leading them away."

Jon interrupted him, "Aye, but the daft mutt led them straight back to us, remember."

"Yep, it has about the same level of intelligence as Beaver, then," said Geoff. "They should get along brilliantly. What are you going to call him?" Ian mused for a while.

"Horace! He's definitely a Horace. That's what I'll call him." There was a general consensus that Horace was a stupid name, but Ian stuck to his guns. He confirmed it when he shouted out the name and the dog eventually, when it had removed itself from the sofa, ambled slowly into the kitchen and sat with his head resting on Ian's lap and went back to sleep.

"Look!" he said triumphantly, "Horace it is. Look at him, he is like a coiled spring, ready to pounce at a moment's notice."

The situation outside the front looked hopeless, the zombies were showing no signs of moving and continued to push against both the van and the bus. Simon and Alex checked out the rear of the property. The garden, being surrounded by a brick wall, was secure, but the alleyway that led between the rear of their gardens and the ones on the next road was full of them. There was no way out that way.

The group did not despair. They'd fought against hundreds of the undead and survived. They had food to last for at least a few weeks and they were in a secure house.

They all agreed that the best course of action was to remain as quiet as possible and to hunker down and see what the next few days brought. It was their only realistic option.

As darkness fell, the group moved into the rear living room and settled down.

Ian was last in. He was carrying a few bottles of whisky and a pack of cards.

"Who's for a Poker marathon? I am going to kick all your butts into the ground and empty your wallets."

They now numbered eight and a dog.

CHAPTER FIFTEEN

Dartmoor

Tiredness eventually broke the group up and they moved inside. The ladies claimed the comfy sofas and armchairs, while the men picked an area of the floor to sleep on.

Simon and Dave organised the guard rota, deciding it would be safer to patrol in twos. The company would keep the sentries more alert and if any zombies found them and possibly breached the perimeter, the adage 'safety in numbers' made the precaution a sensible one.

Despite everyone's protests, Maud insisted on being included in the guard rota.

"I don't care what you all say. I am part of this group and I still have eyes and ears that work. I love cooking and caring for the children, but if me keeping guard for an hour or two allows one of you to get much-needed rest to keep your strength for fighting, then I am helping to keep us safe too."

The protests stopped when, to the amazement of all, she walked over to where the guns were propped up against a wall. She picked one up and deftly performed the safety drill, picked up a loaded magazine and inserted it into the rifle and with a pull, charged the rifle and slung it over her shoulder.

"We were not just cooking, you know. I got young Jim to show me one end of a gun from the other earlier. Come on, Willie, you can accompany me on the first shift." She looked around at the bemused faces staring at her.

"The rest of you get some sleep."

"Young lady," Willie said, chuckling, "it would be my honour to accompany you." Swiftly donning his coat, he picked up his shotgun, linked his arm through hers and they walked out of the door.

As soon as the door was closed, Becky said in a mock whisper.

"Well I think we know who the true leader of this group is." Simon threw the list he had just drawn up into the fireplace and snorted in mock disgust.

"Bloody leader or not, I have to do the blinkin' rota again now!"

The temptation to stay asleep in the morning as the first rays of sunlight shone through the window of the cottage was strong, but I knew the ten more minutes' sleep my body craved wouldn't help, so reluctantly I went to the kitchen and putting the kettle on the gas stove, made myself a coffee. The smell of fresh filter coffee slowly started to wake the others, who yawning, groaning and stretching aching muscles, gathered one by one around the kitchen table.

Soon the delicious smells of bacon cooking filled the room as Maud and Jim made a mound of butties, which we all feasted on. Sarah, after a trying day being shaken around in the trailer, had had a full night's sleep and was in a happy mood, her giggles and laughter as Willie played peek a boo with her making everyone smile.

The first priority of the day was to complete the repairs and improvements to both vehicles. The tractor and trailer needed only minor improvements to reinforce what had already been constructed. On the other hand, upon surveying the damage to the Volvo, we decided that the best course of action would be to completely remove what Shawn had built and, using the same principles, improve it.

None in the Volvo could forget the terror of being surrounded, arms reaching over the steel sheets, clawing at the glass, contorted evil faces only inches from their own.

Using the materials that Willie had let us use, we had a plan to improve the design and strength of the wedges, both at the front and at the rear of the car, and the steel sheeting surrounding it. There was also enough steel mesh available to cover all the windows.

Firing up the generator, the sounds of drilling and cutting soon filled the air.

With Willie helping Shawn and me, Simon and Dave continued with their crash course in military training for the rest of the group. Fulfilling two tasks, they took them on patrols to both keep guard and to keep drilling them on weapon discipline and fighting techniques.

With the day wearing on and with much still to do, it was clear we would not get all the work done in time for us to leave and make any decent distance before night set in. Broaching the subject with Willie, he had no qualms about extending his hospitality for another night. But he did suggest that we would have time to go to Newton Abbot and check out the gun shop. The route there would take us away from the straight and most logical route to Bristol, so going there today could make our journey to-morrow easier.

The idea put us in a quandary. The benefits of the chance to add to our arsenal were clear, and if we went today it would save us time tomorrow, giving us a better chance of making Bristol, and the hope of finding Shawn's friends and then somewhere safe to shelter for the night.

But did we all go or just take the tractor and trailer, leaving some of our group behind? Splitting our forces was something we had earlier decided was not a good idea for many obvious reasons.

If something happened, the capability of each group to defend itself would be reduced, and there was always the possibility of not finding each other again, if the group staying had to evacuate, or if the group leaving got overrun and killed. The others would never know, and sit, waiting for us to return, guessing why, but not actually knowing why we hadn't.

Calling a meeting to discuss the idea, eventually the pros of going outweighed the cons of not, and the decision to go was agreed. I handed the organisation of the expedition over to the military men and carried on with Shawn and Willie, completing the finishing touches to our vehicles.

The tractor looked similar to before, but we knew the extra reinforcing and protection we had added would make it even more impregnable. A steel cage made of farm gates surrounded the tractor cab, giving the driver more protection and we had im-proved the skirts around both that and the trailer, to hopefully stop bodies going under the wheels.

The Volvo was now completely surrounded with a cage made from mesh panels which would prevent any zombie from reaching the occupants inside, and the front plough was heavily reinforced. We were confident it would have the strength to hold together, even if it needed to do as it had done before, and push the trailer.

The hole in the roof had raised sides on it, making it look like a turret, and a ladder hanging on a bracket between the front plough and the roof could be used for climbing down or if in trouble, up to the trailer if it pulled alongside.

I test drove it around the yard and was pleased with the result. It was a lot heavier and that could be felt by the way it handled, but as the need was for strength and power and not a racing car, the sacrifice of speed and agility would be worth it.

Simon and Dave finished planning for the expedition to the gun shop in the nearby market town of Newton Abbot, and called everyone around.

Dave started the meeting.

"I've decided to only send a few in the tractor. The priority is to protect the main group. No matter how many shooters are in the trailer, if they're surrounded and get stuck as before, they won't be able to fight their way out. They'll need rescuing, so I'll keep the larger part of our force in reserve.

That will also mean our ability to defend this place, if need be, is enhanced."

He looked at me.

"Willie, as he knows the way, will accompany you and Simon in the trailer. Shawn will drive with Louise riding shotgun in the cab. You'll be loaded with a good portion of our ammo and food to last a few days." I interrupted.

"I can't leave Becky and the kids. Separating us is not an option. I just can't do it, I'm sorry Dave."

"I thought you'd say that, but can you listen to why I think it's best?" I nodded and crossed my arms, preparing not to agree to whatever he said next.

"You, Simon and Willie in the trailer, armed with rifles and shotguns will be able to deal with most of what you should come across. If the way ahead looks too dicey, you will just turn around and head back before you get into trouble. Your family will be protected by Jim, Steve and myself, backed up by everyone else.

That will include your wife, who along with everyone else, will be able to put enough fire downrange to eliminate all but the biggest horde.

"As soon as you leave, we'll start working on Willie's tractor to armour it. Willie's house has shutters on all the downstairs windows, which we can secure from the inside, so we have an initial sanctuary. If things get too bad here and we think we will be overrun, we can use a ladder to climb down into Willie's tractor and trailer, and make an escape to a list of predetermined positions that you'll know about, so you'll be able to find us.

"If you get trapped, the trailer should keep you safe until we mount a rescue mission, using the Volvo and Willie's tractor to come and get you.

If we have to come to get you, everyone will come, and that will bring a lot more firepower to the party and will keep us together.

"Tom, I need you out there. If you don't go, I'll have to replace you with either Jim or Steve, and no disrespect, but they have a lot more training than you and they'll be more use here if

I need them than they would be, firing at point blank range over the side of a trailer at a crowd of those undead bastards. We have the radios. They may not have the range to reach all the way, but within a few miles of each other, we should be able to communicate clearly. If you get into trouble, we can get close enough to communicate and update the plans if necessary. Also, as soon as you head back and reach the high ground of the moors, we should be able to communicate and let you know if we're in trouble."

I was silent for a long time, thinking it over. The thought of leaving my family, even for a few hours, was terrifying. I made my mind up when I looked at Becky. She stood wearing a tactical vest stuffed with spare mags, rifle over her shoulder and a pistol in a holster strapped to her leg. She nodded at me and mouthed, "It's okay."

"Are you sure?" I asked.

"Tom, I don't want us to be apart, but I can see the sense in what Dave is saying. And we're all able to fight, even Maud, so I have no doubt we can look after ourselves. We need what might be in the gun shop to keep protecting our children, so I think the risk is worth it."

Decision made, I looked at Dave. "Let's go then."

Ten minutes later, I fiercely hugged my wife and children and climbed into the trailer.

Five slowly drove down the track leading to the road.

CHAPTER SIXTEEN

The route Willie had planned used small narrow lanes and tracks to avoid most of the small villages and hamlets on the route. Every house we passed lay silent, shut with no signs of life or with doors left open, indicating a panicked departure. The closer we got to the main A38 trunk road, though, the more signs of life we encountered, or more accurately, signs of death. Cars and vans lay abandoned or crashed, some with their occupants still thrashing inside, unable to escape the restraints of their seat belts; some wandering aimlessly, looking for their next meal, until attracted by the noise of the tractor. The ones we could reach were either pulverised by the plough, or stabbed through the head by one of us with a spear.

This was the first time Willie had seen first-hand the apocalyptic world we had been fighting to survive in for the last few days. Once he had gone through the shock and realisation that it was actually all true, he began to sing a Gaelic war song as he thrust and stabbed at any zombie skull within reach.

Shawn stopped the tractor and turned off the engine when we reached the junction with the A38. The planned route took us straight across it to join another narrow lane that wound its way to our destination. With dismay, we could see a van on its side, blocking our intended route with a small crowd of zombies gathered around it. Loud squawking and screeching from what sounded like a lot of chickens came from the van. None of the zombies noticed our arrival, all too intent on reaching the meal they knew the cacophony of sound indicated.

Louise slid the rear window of the tractor open, so we could plan the next move. Simon patted me on the shoulder.

"Right then, Tom. This is what we're going to do. You're getting the easy job of climbing down to attach a chain to that van, so that we can pull it out of the way. While you're doing that, the rest of us will be risking our lives by standing up here, thinning them out a bit and trying to keep them away from you."

My response made even Simon blink, but knowing I was the obvious choice, I shrugged, smiled grimly and checked my weapons were all ready, while Willie lowered the ladder.

As I stepped off the ladder, I lifted my rifle to my shoulder and gave a quick thumbs-up to Shawn, who started the tractor and edged forward. The noise of the engine starting made most of the zombies turn in my direction.

The rifle in my hands gave me a sense of security. You could kill from a distance and not have to kill up close and personal as we'd had to do at the start, using knives and axes. The red dot on the sights made aiming easier. Moving forward, keeping in line with the bucket on the tractor, as soon as a head centred on the dot, I pulled the trigger. In the periphery of my vision, I could see zombies falling as Willie, Simon and Louise shot and killed the ones nearest to me.

Booms of the shotgun and the loud cracks of rifle fire echoed across the countryside as the zombies fell from the sustained and accurate fire. I could hear Simon and Willie calling shots and magazine changes. Louise, with an open cartridge bag across her shoulder, kept up a withering rate of fire from her shotgun, the blasts of heavy shot causing more damage the closer we got.

Shawn honked the horn on the tractor to indicate we were close enough, so with a final shot at the nearest zombie to me, I let the rifle drop on its sling and grabbed the chain we had shackled to the tractor bucket for this very purpose.

With the van being on its side, it was easy to hook the chain around the rear axle.

I stepped back and waved to Shawn that we were good to go, then I raised my rifle once again, searching for my next target. There were a lot more of them than we had originally thought, but the plan was working, and they were being held back by the rate of fire we could put down. I was shocked when I pulled the trigger and nothing happened.

"I'm out," I called, "Changing mags." I didn't know if this was the correct phrase, but I'd heard it many times in movies. Ejecting the magazine, I grabbed one from a pouch on my vest, when I heard Simon shout.

"Fuck! I'm jammed."

As I turned to look, I fumbled with the fresh magazine and dropped it. With Simon not shooting, the rate of fire had decreased dramatically. This, combined with the movement of the trailer as Shawn reversed, made accuracy difficult, with the result that the horde, rather than being held back, were advancing rapidly towards me.

I looked around. I wouldn't have time to make the ladder before they were on me. My rifle was empty and impotent without a magazine. That left me with one option: my pistol.

Willie had increased his rate of fire to compensate for Simon, who I could hear swearing loudly as he tried to free the empty bullet casing that was jamming his weapon. I could now hear two shotguns firing as Shawn, having realised I was in real trouble, had stopped the tractor. He was standing with Louise on the platform we'd created on its high wheel arches, and he was pouring lead down on the ones closest to me.

My pistol bucked in my hand at every shot. I knew it contained seventeen rounds and I probably wouldn't have time for a reload, so I tried to aim every shot carefully. I stood my ground, balanced, and held it the way Simon and Dave had shown us. The zombies were a mere few feet away, which in a way worked in my favour, as it was difficult to miss despite the panic coursing through my veins. I knew I was down to five shots left when Simon bellowed.

"Tom. Stand back. You're blocking our fire." Hoping this meant he had cleared his rifle, I could do nothing but trust him, and do what he said.

As soon as I'd stepped two paces back, two assault rifles and two shotguns firing as fast as they could decimated the front rank of zombies. I stood dumbly for a few seconds, watching heads explode and holes blasted in bodies from the devastating barrage from above my head.

"Shit, you idiot," I said to myself as I remembered I still had an empty rifle and a pistol with only five shots left. I changed the magazine in my pistol and this time successfully inserted a fresh one in my rifle, and then added my firepower to the fray.

It was impossible for me to see from my position on the ground how many more there were, so I just kept firing and reloading when my rifle clicked empty. All I knew was that the zombies kept coming and they were getting closer.

My ears were ringing from the concussion of the rifles and shotguns firing behind me. I'd just shot the last zombie as it was crawling towards me, with bloody stumps where its legs should have been. From the angle it was coming at me, I shot it through the top of its head, the high velocity bullets tearing through its skull and continuing down through its body.

It wasn't until I'd emptied an entire magazine into it, leaving an unrecognisable pile of blood and bones on the blood-soaked ground that I thought I could hear someone screaming. A few moments later I thought, *"That's me screaming."* It then dawned on me through the red mist of battle that had descended on me, that mine was the only gun that had been firing for some time.

I looked around at the corpses, some still twitching, piled up and forming a semi-circle around me where I stood with my back to the trailer.

Dropping another empty magazine from my gun, I reached for another and inserted it, charging the gun ready for any more that appeared. Hearing voices coming through the ringing in my ears, I looked up to where everyone was looking at me from the tractor and trailer. I couldn't hear what they were saying, so I shook my head to try to clear the fuzz that was filling it.

I heard myself say, "Did we get them all?" The voice sounded distant and echoed. Simon must have realised I was still partially deaf, and held his thumbs up and nodded. He gave a big grin and pointed at the ladder Willie was lowering over the side of the trailer. Grabbing the rungs, I hauled myself up and Willie and

Simon helped me over the side. Willie held his canteen of water out and I drank from it thirstily, and then he handed me a hip flask. The sting of single malt whisky sliding down my throat bought me partially back to my senses.

"Why are you all looking at me?"

"Och, laddie, that was a beautiful thing to watch. I've seen it a few times in my life and I thought I would never see it again."

"Seen what? What the hell are you on about?"

"The Gods of war took hold of you. You started screaming and hollering and every shot you took hit. There was nothing for us to do. You got the last twenty or so all by yourself, we couldn't beat you to the shot." He raised his hip flask to me in a salute.

"You are a true warrior now, my friend. If your back's to the wall and all is looking lost, I would be proud to fight by your side."

Embarrassed by the description of what I'd done, all I could say was, "I don't remember it that way. I didn't even know I was screaming until I heard myself through the ringing in my ears. Anyway, hadn't we better get moving again? You can tell me all about it later, but every minute we're out here is another minute away from my family."

"Yes, mate," Simon said, "but first, let me go and unhook the chain and collect all your dropped mags. I think we may be needing to keep as many as we can before the week's out."

I looked at Shawn, who gave me a big grin and stepped back into the cab of the tractor. He waited until Simon had climbed back up and the ladder hauled up again, before reversing the tractor pulling the still squawking van clear of the road we needed to take.

Simon passed me all the empty magazines, telling me to sit down and reload them all while he and Willie kept watch. After loading the first few from the open ammunition can, I started to calm down and feel normal again. The act of concentrating on pushing the bullets one at a time into the magazines took all my efforts, while the trailer rocked and swayed as it continued its journey.

I looked up and caught Simon looking at me. I knew then why he had me do it. I smiled at him and he just winked and turned back to looking outwards, searching for danger.

Newton Abbot is a sizeable town, but fortunately the gun shop was on a road leading into it. Gun shops, being a destination business and so not needing to attract passing trade, didn't need to be in the expensive town centre retail areas where rents would be higher. Willie's route led us round the small roads surrounding the town, missing most of the residential areas until it was no longer possible, and then we turned onto a road leading straight into the town.

Fires could be seen burning in many parts of Newton Abbot. Shawn had to start using the tractor's bucket to clear abandoned and crashed cars out of the way. Small clusters of zombies stumbled towards us, so we thrust our spears at the ones Shawn missed crushing.

"Not far now," warned Willie. "It's just around the next bend."

"I can hear gun shots!" I exclaimed as the booms of a shotgun being fired could be heard over the engine noise.

"Someone's beaten us to it," growled Willie, "Stay low, we don't know if they'll be friendly or not." He looked at the Tractor.

"Shawn and Louise are mighty exposed in that big cab. It may be zombie-proof, but it ain't bullet proof. Keep a sharp look-out and if it doesn't look right, just fire at it."

I nodded and, gripping my rifle tightly, scanned through the sights for any signs of a threat. The shotgun fell silent as we rounded the corner. Ahead, a large crowd of hundreds of zombies pressed against the front of a shuttered shop. It was a two-storey building with a flat roof. A sign proudly emblazoned across the front, announced it was the shop we were looking for. Bodies lay in piles between the surging crowd.

"On the roof," warned Simon, and we all aimed our weapons at a figure holding a shotgun who was waving in our direction. Simon waved back.

"He looks friendly enough. Keep your guns on him just in case, but fingers off triggers."

"Try and thin them out a bit with the plough," Simon shouted to Shawn, "Do a few passes and then we'll finish the rest off."

Shawn put the tractor in gear and pressed the accelerator, changing rapidly up through the gears and gaining as much speed as he could out of the heavy vehicle. The plough hit the crowd with huge momentum, and some bodies simply burst apart while others were pulverised under the blade. The ones on the edges of the swathe he cut were thrown aside, as the shock of the impact hitting the leading ones spread through the pack. Driving clear through to the other side, he continued down the road until there was space to swing around and then, foot to the floor, he built up speed to smash through them again.

Twice more he cut a path through them until there were very few left standing. Every time the tractor and trailer cleared the crowd, the man on the roof started firing at the ones left behind, thinning them out some more.

It was impossible to shoot from the trailer as it was bouncing around so much, so all we could do was just hold on and watch the destruction Shawn was causing. Hundreds of the undead lay pulverised, many still jerking and twitching, their mangled, ruined corpses unable to move from where they had been cast aside by the plough.

"Get as close to the shop front as you can," Simon shouted to Shawn through the rear window of the cab. Shawn slowed down and steered the tractor as close to the shop front as possible.

Lowering the plough so it scraped on the tarmac pavement, the plough pushed the remaining zombies aside. The ones squeezed between the plough and the brick wall and steel shutters of the shop built up to a mound of crushed, twitching unrecognisable pile of groaning offal.

It was almost peaceful when Shawn turned the tractor's engine off, only the low groaning and rasping of the remaining zombies to disturb a beautiful day.

"Am I glad to see you!" said the man on the roof as he peered over to look at us. Willie extended the ladder to reach the roof and called up.

"Permission to come aboard?"

"No problem," he replied, "I'll steady the ladder for you."

We climbed up one by one, and he held out his hand to assist us all over the low brick parapet that surrounded the roof.

"Ah know you. You're the wee lad that works here, aren't you?" growled Willie in his gruff Scottish accent. He held out his hand and shook the hand of the young man standing in front of him. "I'm Willie Beedie from Tor Farm up on the moors. Ah get my cartridges and stuff from here. It's good to see ya made it, laddie."

"Yes, yes. I remember you. I'm Shane Casey. We don't get many accents like yours around here. You buy home loading stuff, if I remember rightly."

"Too right. I'm not buying that expensive stuff you sell, I'd rather make my own." I introduced the rest of us, and handshakes were exchanges all round. Shane looked exhausted. A few rifles and shotguns leant against the wall and the roof was littered with spent cartridges and bullet casings. A hatch with a ladder poking out of the top was in the corner of the roof.

Louise handed him a mug of coffee from a flask she produced from the rucksack on her back. He gratefully accepted it and sat down, leaning his back against the wall, the mug cupped in in his hands.

"I'm so glad to see you guys. I've been here for days thinking I was the only person left alive in the world. When me and the boss saw what was happening outside, at first we thought it was a riot or something. It was crazy, people were running and screaming, cars were driving madly everywhere. And then they came. Attacking everyone and eating them as we watched. We pulled down the shutters and hid. After listening to the radio and watching social media on our phones, we slowly figured out that somehow everyone had turned into zombies. We didn't know what the hell to do."

"Where's your boss?" I asked.

"I don't know. After the first few hours when it was clear no one was coming to help, Ian left to go and get his family. He took a couple of guns and a bag of cartridges and went out the back door. I haven't seen him since. All I know is about half an hour after he left, there was a flurry of shots not far away and then silence. I was in complete panic and kept running around the shop, rechecking that every door and window was locked.

"Then I remembered the ladder that led to the roof, so I thought I'd go and see if anyone was out there. It was then I knew everything was lost."

He went silent and bowed his head, tears dripped down his nose and he began sobbing.

"I looked over the edge and my whole family was in the street. My mom, my dad and my little brother. I shouted to them and was about to run down and open the doors to let them in when I noticed they weren't acting normal.

They were staggering aimlessly, but when they heard my shout, they came towards the shop. I knew it was too late. All of them were covered in blood and had turned into those things down there.

"I spent the next day looking at them, going out of my mind. Twice I almost lost it and jumped off the roof so I could join them, but something stopped me. Then I got angry, screaming and shouting at the unfairness of it all. The noise I was making attracted more and soon a crowd of them surrounded the shop. I spent hours shouting at them, blaming them all for killing my family. That was when I realised I could get my revenge. it was those bastards down there that had killed my family and I wanted to kill them. I went back into the shop got some shotguns and rifles and plenty of ammunition and I've spent the last few days killing as many as I could."

I peered over the edge at all the corpses scattered in windrows on the street below.

"Where are your family now?" I asked softly. He looked up.

"They were the first I shot. I knew they weren't coming back and the thought of them remaining as they were, that wasn't how I wanted to remember them."

He waved his hand towards the street.

"They're underneath that lot somewhere, but at least I know they're at peace now." Simon stepped forward and put his hand on his shoulder.

"You are one brave man. The reason we're here, though, is to raid your shop."

He then told Shane about our group and what we'd been through in the last few days, and also about the plan we had agreed on to make our way to Warwick castle, picking up friends and relatives on the way. He ended by saying to Shane,

"The problem is that, as you are here, I see you as the rightful owner of everything this shop contains. Now, I've never stolen anything in my life and I'm not about to start now. I can only ask if we can take some supplies with us." He paused.

"I can also ask if you would like to join us. I'm not sure if you have anyone else you'd like to try and find. If you have, I can't promise anything other than if we can get to them, we'll do our best to make it happen." Shane didn't hesitate.

"Yes. I want to join your group," he said immediately, "If you hadn't turned up I would have starved to death eventually. I owe you my life. I don't really have any family I'm close to nearby. I have an aunt and uncle in Birmingham, I know roughly where they live from memory, but I doubt you'd want to risk heading into a big city. Just look at what this little town was like.

As far as I'm concerned, everything in the shop below is yours to take. It's not really mine anyway, and I think Ian's dead now, so there's no one who can claim it's theirs." Willie helped him to his feet.

"Let's not waste another second, then. Shall we go and empty the sweet shop?"

The shop was dark, with little light seeping through the shutters. Shane went to a shelf that contained hunting lamps and torches. Turning them on, he placed them around the shop, illuminating the whole place.

It wasn't the biggest gun shop I'd been in, but the walls still held an impressive number of shotguns and rifles.

"What shall we take?" asked Shane. Four voices responded in unison.

"Everything!"

When we saw the quantity of shotgun cartridges in the storeroom, we had a planning meeting to work out the best and easiest way to get it all on to the roof and back down into the trailer. We didn't want to leave anything behind. As far as we knew, this could be our last chance to get weapons and ammunition. It didn't take much to calculate that due to the amount of ammunition we'd expended over the last few days, there could never be a limit to what was enough. If it was there, we just had to take it.

Passing the rifles and shotguns up was the easiest part of the job, because we formed a chain and passed them from hand to hand. The rifle ammunition wasn't too difficult either. Shane found a few large bags and emptied the strongboxes holding all their stock of rifle ammunition. Tying a rope around the handles, we hauled them up too, and added them to the large stack of weapons on the roof.

The shotgun cartridges were another matter altogether. They were just plain heavy. A slab of two hundred and fifty cartridges is fine on its own. Carrying two slabs together is something you only wanted to do over a short distance. The storeroom held tens of thousands of cartridges of all gauges and shot weights.

There was nothing else to do but get on with it, so while Shane and Louise emptied the shelves and storeroom of anything else of value, the four of us made trip after trip, hauling the invaluable cartridges up to the roof.

We kept an eye out on the street below, where a few more zombies had joined the couple that had missed our attentions earlier, but the numbers so far did not pose a great problem.

Loading the trailer was a quicker affair. Willie, Simon and Shawn climbed into the trailer and we threw everything down to them. Not having time to neatly stack what was being passed to them, the jumble of goods spread across the bed of the trailer. It might make for an uncomfortable journey back, but that was a small price to pay for what we'd collected.

When the last few items had been passed down, I surveyed what we'd gathered. Apart from the guns and ammunition, we had a large collection of knives, clothing, torches and even a few boxes of ready to eat food pouches that were the civilian equivalent to the military's MREs. Willie got excited when he saw the volume of home loading machines and components they had stored at the shop, and he promised to show us all how to use them when we got back.

The final items Shane gathered were the tools from the small gunsmith workshop the business had. He explained that they did most gun repairs themselves, and Ian, the owner, had been training him in the basics of gunsmithing.

Shane proved to be a pleasant young man. He had worked at the shop since leaving college and loved working there. Being a hunting and shooting enthusiast himself, he said working in the industry that he enjoyed, and the contacts he made in the shop made following his passion easier. And he joked that having staff discount on all the products made his hobby a lot cheaper too.

With nothing left to keep us there, I was desperate to get back to my family, so I was urging everyone to hurry up and get on board our mobile castle. Shawn fired up the tractor, set the plough to the right level and set off back to the moors.

Six now set off, following the route five had taken a few hours previously.

CHAPTER SEVENTEEN

Even though I knew we were still out of range, I continually kept trying to raise the farm on the radio as we wove our way down the narrow lanes leading away from Newton Abbot. If something had happened to them and I hadn't been there, I knew I would never forgive myself. Despite constant reassurances from both Simon and Willie about being too far away and that my family were more than capable of looking after themselves, I knew I couldn't relax until I saw them.

Simon and Shane busied themselves sorting through what we had taken from the gun shop. When Simon found a box of the right calibre rifle ammunition, he loaded one of his magazines with it.

Spotting a zombie stumbling along the side of the road, a man with half his face chewed off and his entrails falling out of the gaping wound in his stomach, he shouted for Shawn to stop the tractor.

"I want to see what difference using expanding ammunition makes," he explained. Steadying his aim, he fired at the former man slowly staggering towards us. His first shot was aimed at the shoulder. The force of the shot knocked it backwards, spinning it around as it fell to the ground. What was left of its arm was held on by a few scraps of bone and tissue.

"That's better," he exclaimed. "Willie was right, these babies have a lot more stopping power that the .556 we've been using." He aimed his next shot at the thrashing zombie, who with one arm now useless, was trying to stand up. The back of its skull disappeared in a red mist of blood, brains and bone.

"Shane, how many rounds of .223 do you think we have?"

"Not that many, I'm afraid. It's not that popular a calibre. We sell mostly .308 and .243 for deer stalking. We should have plenty of components to be able to manufacture thousands, though." Shane, Simon and Willie then started a long conversation about the different calibres and what each thought would be the best zombie-killing one to use.

All the talk of different calibres, grains of powder to use, and muzzle velocity was lost on me, as my knowledge of firearms was limited to shotguns and the .22 rimfire that I'd been using. It was something I was sure I would pick up by necessity, but for the moment all I cared about was that the huge pile of equipment we had would be instrumental in helping keep us alive.

Only a few zombies were encountered on the way back to the farm and these we easily killed by either running them over or using our spears. Shane insisted on wielding a spear alongside us in the trailer, stating simply that he blamed every one of them for the death of his family, and each one he killed would be one less for him to face later.

The journey passed quickly as the road had already been cleared of obstructions by us earlier, so Shawn was able to set a reasonably fast pace.

Eventually I got a crackled response from my repeated radio calls. The signal got clearer the closer we got, until at long last I got an intelligible response. To my immense relief, they were all fine, had had no issues apart from being worried sick at the length of time we'd been away.

As the sun began to sink over the horizon, I told them we were about half an hour away and to get the kettle on.

Our homecoming was like a victory parade. Pulling into the yard, we were surrounded by everyone cheering and clapping, celebrating our safe return.

I could not climb fast enough down the ladder and into the embrace of my wife and children.

I was as probably as guilty as most in sometimes taking my relationship with my wife and children lightly. Why not? They were always going to be there for me, and arguments soon blew over and forgiveness was something I knew would eventually achieve, whatever misdemeanour had occurred.

But now. With the knowledge that the next moment could either be my last, or the last moment for one of my family, it made me really appreciate the love that I held for them. The small niggles and trivialities of life that caused cross words to be spoken just did not seem relevant at all now.

As soon as the reunions were all complete, Shane was introduced to everyone.

"So, what did you manage to get then?" Dave asked. Simon walked to the rear door of the trailer, opened the locking bar and with a heave, swung one of the doors wide open. Dave stood staring at the huge pile of guns, ammunition and the host of other goods we had collected. He spluttered a few times, unable to get the words out, until eventually summing up his thoughts with, "Fuck me. That'll do."

It was a happy band that gathered around Willie's kitchen table a short while later, eating another delicious meal cooked by Maud. The achievements of the day, in improving the protection around the Volvo and tractor, the training that everyone had gone through to improve gun knowledge, fighting skills and techniques, culminating in a successful mission to gather more guns and ammunition, and the addition of another member to the group, gave everyone a real sense of accomplishment.

Today was the first day when we were not just running away, our only aim to survive for as long as we could.

We had proved to ourselves that it was possible to do more than just that, and we had been proactive not just reactive to situations. Even though we had only been together for a few days, the bonds between everyone were growing strong, and even though we were practically a stranger to one another, it did feel as if we'd had known them for years.

The only thought that did put a dampener on the whole affair, was that in the morning, we needed to leave this sanctuary we had found and continue with our plans to reach Warwick castle.

Tomorrow the whole group would be facing unknown dangers. I looked at Becky and at the sea of faces around the table and thought that the one consolation was that at least we would face them together.

When the table had been cleared and the kids coaxed into bed, we set about organising the trailer, the task being made easier by many willing hands. Using the generator, we took the risk to set up some portable lights, making the job easier than fumbling around under torchlight.

Becky, Maud, Louise and Lucy took one look at Dave's and my attempt to put it all back on in a neat and orderly fashion, and they ordered us to stop, and relegated us to the role of porters. In no time at all the sub floor was filled to the brim with items tightly packed together. Other more essential items were stacked neatly at the front of the trailer.

Most of the spare guns were laid on top before the floor was put back into place. Shawn constructed a rudimentary gun rack, fixed to the side of the trailer, to hold the ones we wanted to keep to hand, with an open-topped box by its side to store a large quantity of cartridges and ammunition, to make them readily available.

We kept the boot space in the Volvo clear so that if we came across more supplies, they could be loaded quickly. The only items we packed in it were some spare guns, a stack of ammunition, our spears and a small emergency rucksack for everyone containing survival items and food.

Despite Willie's protests, we insisted he help himself to anything he wanted. It was only when I pointed out that he could give them, if he wanted to, to other survivors he might come across, that he relented and picked out a selection of rifles and shotguns and a quantity of ammunition for them.

After it was all completed, we all slumped exhausted into the chairs we had brought out from the house, and we sat in a circle with the lamp in the middle, as we had done the previous night. Shane fitted in with the group well and wasn't shy about putting his point of view forward or suggesting other ways to do things.

The whisky bottle that was passed around mellowed everyone's mood. Maud didn't notice Willie topping up her glass, and she got a little tipsy. She began to tell us dirty jokes, which had us all splitting our sides with laughter. When she began telling us of her love for us all, Becky insisted that she go and have a lie down. Returning a few minutes later, she stood before Willie.

"I saw what you were doing. You got her drunk on purpose. That is an unfair and cruel thing to do." Willie laughed and held his hands up in apology.

"Aye, my dear, I did too. And I'll tell you why. I don't think you all know and appreciate how amazing that woman is. She told me what her life was like before this all happened and you met her. Her husband was a cruel, horrible and vindictive little man who made her life a misery. But some of you met him, so you know that already.

"I've been watching her, and not only because I think she's an attractive woman. She is constantly on the go; making sure wee baby Sarah and the kids are happy, the food is cooking and myriad other things you probably don't notice. Don't get me wrong, she wants to do all those things and she can do them very easily, but she needs to let go of the sorrow that has built up inside her from years of neglect.

"Those few drams of whisky I sneaked on her brought out a side of her that has probably never been seen before. The true Maud. Hopefully, now it's come out once, it'll be easier for it to next time. She alone might have persuaded me to come along with you, and she did ask last night when we were patrolling together. But I know my place is on these moors, and no one, not even the godsend that is Maud, will make me leave.

"She needs her rest and would have insisted on patrolling to-night along with the rest of us, because she doesn't know her true worth, and keeps wanting to please you all. Now I bet she's sleeping soundly, and getting the rest she deserves.

And that, young lady, is why I gave her a few extra drams of the elixir of life."

We all sat there, thinking about what he had said. I fully expected Becky to argue the point some more, but instead she stepped forward and gave Willie a hug. She still had tears in her eyes when a few minutes later, she released him from her embrace and sat back down. Dave was looking at Willie with a mock puzzled look.

"Are you a bloody psychologist now?" Willie held his glass up.

"No, laddie, just a true believer in the power of a good dram of Isle of Skye single malt."

The laughter brought us back to the present and the next hour was spent patrolling the perimeter and sharing good whisky with good friends, before tiredness forced us to head to sleep.

We were now twenty-three.

CHAPTER EIGHTEEN

My watch shift had been the middle of the night shift, and I was tired, following the broken night's sleep. But that was dispelled by the huge breakfast and mugs of fresh coffee that Maud produced from the kitchen.

As the last few items were being loaded, I helped Shawn put the last few finishing touches to the work the others had done yesterday to Willie's tractor and trailer. It wasn't as big and new as the one we had. Nevertheless, it would give him the extra protection needed when he had to leave the farm.

Unable to draw the moment out any longer, the time to leave arrived. We again thanked Willie profusely for all the unconditional help and shelter he had selflessly provided us with. He waved it away, saying it was nothing and anyone would have done the same. We knew differently.

Following handshakes from the men, he was beaming with pleasure from all the hugs and kisses the women gave him. Maud was last in line. She first shook his hand, telling him to be careful and not to do anything stupid. She turned away to climb into the trailer, but stopped and whirling round, grabbed him by the shoulders. Wrapping her arms around him, she gave him a long and from what I could see, passionate kiss. When she released him, he staggered slightly, a bemused, shocked look on his face. Then he burst out laughing and bellowed to the world.

"What did I tell you? The power of a good single malt. You all take care of that fantastic woman, you hear me, or you will answer to me, and God help you if I catch you." We all guffawed with laughter. Maud, not quite understanding why, tried to look embarrassed, but her face kept cracking into a joyful smile.

We were as ready as we were ever going to be, so with a last wave and shouted farewells, the small convoy drove out of Willie's yard and along the track that led to the road to start our journey to Bristol, where we hoped to find Shawn's friends.

For no other reason than it had worked before, everyone assumed the same positions they'd had earlier in the vehicles. Shane joined the ones in the trailer. When Dave had given him an SA80 rifle and a pistol in a holster to clip round his waist, he could not fail to show his boyish excitement at having the opportunity to use them. Being familiar with a wide variety of firearms, it didn't take much explaining on their use for him to fully grasp their operation.

The now familiarly empty roads didn't bother us as we followed the route we had planned. We were first going to try the main A38, which then joined the M5 at Exeter. If it was passable, it would be the most direct route to take. If we discovered the way was blocked, then the wide carriageway would give us enough room to turn around and attempt one of the secondary routes. Shawn and I both carried maps marked with all the alternative routes we had planned, so all it would take was a quick radio call and we would both know which route to follow next if we had to deviate. After clearing a path through the carnage we had come across further down the A38 a few days before, we knew what the vehicles were capable of, so we were not too worried about getting stuck. We could just turn around and keep trying routes until, hopefully, we found a clear one. Although we didn't want to find ourselves as we had at the base, hemmed in by an impassable horde of the undead.

Exeter worried us. It was the largest population centre in the area and the M5 motorway skirted around the outer edge of it.

The motorway would have been the obvious escape route that most would have headed for, so we didn't hold out much hope of it being clear. But we did hope that we would be able to work our way through whatever we found. We had agreed not to risk it if there was a large gathering of zombies, and to just turn around.

The first few miles passed reasonably uneventfully, with only the odd car to clear out of the way, and the accompanying zombies to exterminate. Everyone's hopes raised when we pulled out onto the A38 ten miles south of Exeter and found it to be clear.

Shawn increased his speed until he reached what we had discovered was the optimum for the passengers in the trailer: twenty-five miles per hour. Any faster and the ride got too uncomfortable.

I was puzzled when Shawn slowed down when passing an abandoned articulated lorry. Reaching level to the cab, he stopped. The radio crackled to life.

"I think we should try and get some fuel from the lorry. There's nothing in sight and it could be our best chance for a while."

My fuel gauge had dropped to half-full. The slow speeds we were driving at, and the extra weight my car was carrying didn't make for an economical drive. We did have full jerrycans stored in the trailer from the fuel we'd scavenged from the tanks at Bickley barracks, but the sense of replenishing our supplies at every opportunity was better.

"Good call, mate," I replied. "Have you had a chance to look at the name on the side of the lorry?" The name of one of the main UK supermarkets was emblazoned along the side.

"While we're emptying its tank, it would be a shame not to see what's inside it as well," Shawn chuckled over the radio.

"How did I miss that? I'm the one who's supposed to be a prepper." I spoke to Dave beside me.

"You and Simon are in charge now. You keep guard and we'll see what we can find."

"Right you are, then," he replied.

"Simon, leave Jim in the trailer on overwatch. You and me on perimeter security and everyone else can muck in. Fair enough?" Dave suggested. Simon gave a thumbs-up, and lowered the ladder over the side. Chet unhooked our ladder, put it in position and climbed down. The rest of us followed and stretching our aching muscles, we waited for the others to climb down from the trailer one by one.

Simon and Dave checked the surrounding area and declared it clear. The children, much to their disappointment, were told to stay in the trailer. Dave mollified them somewhat by telling them he needed their young eyes constantly watching for danger to keep us safe.

Shawn broke the filler cap off the lorry's fuel tank and peered inside. Announcing it was three-quarters full, he set up the small hand pump he'd found at the workshop, and he started pumping out fuel into an empty jerrycan. Steve stood by, holding another jerrycan and a funnel, waiting for the first to be filled so he could pour it into our fuel tanks.

I used a crowbar to break the lock on the rear shutter doors of the lorry, releasing the catch to allow the door to roll up on its springs. It was full of pallet after pallet of foodstuff of all descriptions.

There was clearly too much to take, but following Shawn's mantra of 'If it's there, take it', Becky and I climbed into the rear of the lorry to decide quickly what would be best to take.

Tins of meat, vegetables, fruit and packets of dried food such as pasta were the obvious choices, so wasting no time we ripped open the wrapping surrounding the pallets and started handing down slabs of food.

We had designed the protective shield around the Volvo, so the boot could still be opened for incidents such as this. In no time the chain of people passing the items from hand to hand had filled it completely, the added weight making it sink even lower on its suspension.

Getting the goods into the trailer was a little more difficult, with someone having to stand half-way up the ladder, passing up to another leaning over the side. The effort was worth it, though, as the food we were loading, combined with what we already had should be enough to feed us for weeks.

A shout from Eddie of 'Zombies coming' stopped all work in its tracks.

A small group was approaching along the road from the direction we had come from. Dave had been watching in that direction, but Eddie's young eyes had beaten him to it.

The group didn't panic. We could see there weren't enough of them to trouble us, but their arrival indicated that it was probably a good time to leave. Our fuel supplies had been replenished, and we had added a lot of food to our inventory. There was no point pushing our luck anymore, so Dave ordered everybody back into the vehicles.

Just as Becky and I were about to climb down from the lorry, she stopped and scrambled over a few full pallets to reach one near the back. She returned clutching a few boxes of sweets.

"May as well get the kids some treats," she grinned as she passed them over to me.

"Nice one, love. Not sure what Maud will think, though."

"Oh, I'm sure she understands the power a pack of Jelly Babies can hold over a whining child," she said as she climbed up the ladder and reached down to take the boxes off me.

I grinned as I could hear the excited shouts from young throats when they saw what Becky was carrying.

Our journey continued.

The dark smear of smoke covering the horizon was a better indication we were nearing Exeter than the signposts telling us how far away we were. More abandoned or crashed vehicles littered the road, but we were able to weave a path through them. Shawn had dropped his speed to a virtual crawl as he chose the best path to take, occasionally stopping, and stepping from the cab so he could survey the road better and pick his route.

The nearer we got to Exeter, the slower we went. Shawn had to start using his bucket to push cars out of the way, and the zombies got more numerous. He was doing a great job and never committed the vehicle to a situation where he would not be able to reverse out or turn around. The slow pace, though, meant that the zombies could keep up with us when we attracted their attention with all the noise we were making.

I kept reversing my car, using the wedge at the rear to keep thinning out the following crowd, and Dave, Chet and Steve were sweating heavily from the exertion of using the steel spears.

The sight of hordes of zombies no longer filled us with dread. If we had a clear way through, we knew we should be safe.

Slowly we weaved our inexorable way onwards, leaving a trail of dead and mangled bodies in our wake.

Occasionally, to avoid any chance of getting trapped, we resorted to using our guns to deal with a larger concentration. The amount of firepower we now had enabled us to scythe through them without any trouble.

As the A38 became the M5 motorway, it widened to three carriageways. Cars and lorries still littered the road, but the extra width enabled us to speed up slightly and leave our entourage of undead fans behind. On a clear patch of road, I pulled up next to Shawn and indicated for him to stop.

The last few hours of relentless exertion had left the passengers in my car exhausted. I was sure the ones in trailer would feel the same way, so would welcome the chance to grab a breather and to drink and eat something.

Flasks of coffee and sandwiches made from delicious fresh bread Maud had baked earlier were handed out and gratefully eaten. I took the chance to climb down and inspect my car for any damage. Apart from the inevitable dents and scrapes, it had stood up to its baptism of fire. Unidentifiable body parts were on various bits of it, and everywhere was coated with a layer of blood.

Simon and Dave reminded everyone to reload empty magazines and check their weapons.

Shane had been wanting to zero in some of the rifles collected from the gun shop since we'd returned, but with all the work involved in sorting out and reloading the vehicles, had never got the chance. When the zombies who had been following us appeared over the low rise in the road behind us, Shane asked Dave about trying some of the weapons out, and he agreed that now would be a good time. The noise we'd been making had any in the area heading for us anyway, so a few gunshots wouldn't affect our situation too adversely.

Simon acted as spotter, using a pair of binoculars to call the fall of shot, while Shane steadied himself. Resting the rifle on the edge of the trailer, he aimed at the approaching horde.

Shane told Simon which one he was aiming at and Simon called the corrections. Working together, it only took three or four shots per rifle to get each on zeroed in accurately enough for our needs, and then a few more shots to make sure. He said he would fine-tune them later, but we all agreed that a head shot from two hundred yards would be accurate enough.

Refreshed from the short break and with the zombies now only one hundred yards away, we set off again, soon leaving our followers behind as we set a steady pace, weaving around the cars and lorries littering the motorway. From how the cars were abandoned, you could work out the untold story of their poor occupants.

A lot were pulled over on the hard shoulder, indicating the driver had probably been suffering from the last stages of the virus. They'd still had enough about them to pull to the side and stop the car safely, in the hope that they would recover and be able to continue. Most of these vehicles still held captive their former owner, thrashing and clawing at its interior, trying to reach us as we slowly drove past.

Other vehicles were parked in the same way, but had their doors open. We imagined that the driver's last act was to get out of the vehicle in the vague hope that fresh air would help. Open doors meant the occupants were loose, which was borne out by the fact that there were usually some cars crashed nearby, as panicked drivers must have tried to avoid the living roadblock created by the freshly turned, inevitably adding themselves to the zombie population. These zombies, trapped by the barriers and fences hemming in the motorway, were no match for our vehicles. Mile by slow mile, we continued, leaving a trail of corpses behind us.

The road was completely blocked just after we passed the last junction for Exeter. Shawn stopped and stepped out of the cab. He announced after a few minutes studying the pile-up that he could see a way through it. The side of the motorway sloped down a hill, so he planned to simply drive along its edge and push out of the way those that blocked the route, and let gravity do the rest. Pulling to the edge of the motorway, you could see the tracks left by other vehicles as the drivers trying to escape the roadblock had used the sloping grass embankment. The steep sides had defeated the efforts of many, their cars ending up rolling or sliding to the bottom, where they lay abandoned.

Happily, some tracks that reached back up the carriageway the far side of the blockage showed successful attempts had been made.

I couldn't tell how old the tracks were, but the thought of others doing as we were, surviving and trying to reach somewhere, filled us with hope.

Sticking as close as I could to the back of the trailer, I followed Shawn as he started to clear the wreckage that lay ahead of us. The solid mass of crunched metal created by the crashed vehicles made it hard for zombies to reach us. Their arms still reached out to us, though, as they futilely tried to negotiate the maze that lay between us.

Thrusts with the spears ended the existence of the ones in our path as Shawn drove deeper into the roadblock. Vehicles rolled or slid down the steep slope as he skilfully used the bucket and power of the tractor to push them aside.

The radio crackled into life.

"Tom, I may need a push soon. There's a big old lorry in the way." A few more cars rolled down the slope until I could see and hear Shawn revving the tractor, its wheels spinning as he tried to push the lorry.

"Hold on, everyone," I shouted, as I nudged the back of the trailer with the wedge at the front of my vehicle.

Pressing my foot on the accelerator, I slowly increased power. The wedge held fast, testament to the way we had constructed it. Inch by inch, we moved, my spinning, smoking wheels filling the air with the pungent smell of burning rubber, until at last the lorry released itself from whatever was holding it back, and we lurched forward. I watched with satisfaction as the lorry slid down the slope before coming to rest against a tree.

Bouncing over metal and other debris laying on the carriageway, I backed off from the trailer and followed as he continued with his demolition job.

"Only a few more to go," broadcast the radio. Moments later we were clear.

The crash had stopped any cars getting further. Looking ahead, the road was clear for as far as I could see. We continued.

The sign advertising a service station in one mile enabled me to get my bearings again. I smiled to myself as it was the one we usually stopped at when we drove to Cornwall. It was a good few hours' drive under normal conditions from our home, and therefore, the coffee I'd usually drunk would have reached my bladder by then. We found the food at the service station was slightly better than the usual overpriced rubbish most offered, and to me the main benefit was that it had a huge carpark, so it was easy to park when towing the caravan.

Becky, having seen the sign too, waved and pointed to it as we passed, smiling as she mouthed, "Do you need the loo?" One of us was usually desperate to go by the time we reached here, so normally one of us was racing across the carpark, desperate to reach the toilets before it was too late.

It had become a joke between the children as they guessed who would be the one running.

Ruefully I thought to myself, "A visit to a motorway service station. Another part of normal life we most likely will never experience again."

CHAPTER NINETEEN

Mile after mile slipped by, albeit slowly due the pace set by Shawn. We had estimated it would take us most of the day to reach Bristol. At the speed we were going and if we hit no more problems, it had been a fair guess.

With no zombies to kill, Dave, Chet and Steve sat down in their seats. For the next few miles we enjoyed the empty road and chatted. Not concentrating fully, as I was explaining to Steve why rugby is a far better sport than football would ever be, I missed seeing some debris in the road. It was a piece of wood, which Shawn, with his high clearance and wide axels had missed. Only seeing it as it emerged from underneath the trailer, I was slow to respond and yanked the wheel over to try and avoid it. The car jolted as my front wheel hit it.

Immediately I knew something was wrong, the steering went heavy and the car started juddering.

"Shit! We've blown a bloody tyre," I exclaimed, furiously stopping the car. I hit the steering wheel, angry with myself, knowing it was my lapse in concentration that had led to this. Picking up the radio, Dave told Shawn to stop.

"Where's the spare?" asked Dave.

"Underneath all that shit in the back. And it's only one of those crappy little temporary ones too. It's going to be a nightmare to change with all the armour we've put on. I don't even know if we can get to the wheel."

"Tom, there's no point moaning about it now. It's happened, and we'll just have to get on with it." He turned to Chet and Steve.

"There ain't no zombies in sight now, but we know that can change. I want you two on perimeter security. Max out your ammo, then stuff some more in and keep sharp."

Shawn had turned the tractor round and pulled up next to me. Climbing down from the cab, he walked over to me, with Louise by his side.

"It's my fault," he said when I told him what had happened, "I saw the lump of wood and it was only when I was on top of it, I thought of you behind me."

I laughed, "Cheers, pal, I'll let you take the blame. I was only just blaming myself. We were chatting and I was slow to see it." He got onto his knees and looked under the steel sheeting.

"We're going to have to remove some of this to get to it. I'll go and get some tools. Tell me you know where your locking wheel nut key is?"

"In the glove box, I hope. The main bloody problem is the spare is one of those temp jobs, and I don't think it'll be up to much," I replied, turning around to climb back into the car. Relieved to find the key was still where I had last seen it, I climbed back out and joined the others, who by now had climbed down from the trailer. Dave spoke to us all.

"Right, same as before. Simon and I will be in charge of security. Shawn, how many do you need to help?"

"If we can have a few to help unload the boot first to get to the spare, then Tom and I should be able to do it. It will probably take us twenty minutes to half an hour to strip the side off, change the wheel and get it all back together."

Looking up the road, a few figures could now be seen in the distance.

"You have fifteen minutes." He looked at Shane. "Sharp-shooter Shane. You'll soon have a chance to show us how good you are. Get back in the trailer and start dropping those as soon as they're in range. Shawn, you stick to changing the wheel, but I may need you to use the tractor to thin those bastards out if we can't hold them back.

Kids, stay in the trailer and keep watch as before.

"The rest of you, grab as much ammo as you can, and set up a tight 360 perimeter. We're deep in enemy territory and have a vehicle down. Until it's fixed, we ain't going anywhere. It's up to us to keep whatever may come at bay."

Simon laughed, "Bloody hell, mate. I remember you saying exactly the same when that truck broke down in Helmand. Shit, that was a fight. Those fucking Taliban kept coming, no matter how many we dropped."

"Yes, mate. But we had Apache helicopters overhead then as well. Now we have four trained soldiers and a bunch of civvies, half of them women. I think I'd rather face the Taliban any day of the week, than a tide of undead bastards who don't feel pain."

Becky looked at him. She stood with her rifle held ready, her vest stuffed with extra magazines.

"Civvies? We are all you have. So, stop moaning and tell us what to do. If you think I'm going to let any of those things past me to get to my kids, then think again. If you think the Taliban were scary, you haven't seen an angry mother."

Victoria, who was standing next to Becky and decked out in the same kit, spoke up.

"Yes, Becky. You men think you can fight. You just watch." Simon laughed and slapped Dave on the back.

"I'll leave you to dig yourself out of this one." Dave huffed and flustered, his face growing red with embarrassment.

"Sorry, ladies. I'm just an old git, that's all. I know you can do it, and you're not just civvies, you're the strongest, bravest women I've met." Becky looked at Victoria, Lucy and Louise.

"Shall we forgive him?"

Maud called down from the trailer. She had a rifle over her shoulder and was holding Sarah on her hip.

"Don't worry, girls. I'll be cooking his food later. We'll see how sorry he is then." He held up his hands in surrender.

The loud bang of Shane firing a rifle from the trailer bought them all back to focus. Sarah began crying at the shock of the sudden noise. Simon called over to Dave.

"I'll go on overwatch with Shane and try and get as many as I can."

Meanwhile, while the boot was emptied of all the supplies we'd loaded earlier, Shawn and I began to remove the side panels from the car. We congratulated ourselves on choosing to bolt the sheets to the frame we'd constructed, rather than weld them on. It had taken longer, but we figured that should we need to repair it, then undoing bolts would be easier than breaking welds.

Sweating and with knuckles bleeding from knocking them against the hard frame, we worked together to undo the bolts.

"Let's find a cordless impact driver, it'll be bloody quicker and less painful," I moaned as I sucked the blood from another bleeding knuckle. Chet carried over the spare wheel and jack, waiting for us to use them.

Simon and Shane were now firing continually. Glancing up at the trailer, I saw Daisy handing Shane a fresh magazine. The hunting rifles only held three bullets, but Shane had chosen ones with removable magazines, so using extra ones he had gathered from the shop, and with the children loading them, they were able to keep up a good rate of fire.

"How far away are they, Chet?"

"Still quite a way. They're getting closer, but Simon and Shane are holding them."

When the sheeting was removed, changing the wheel was a quick job. The thin temporary wheel, though, looked completely out of place and inadequate for the job.

"The first XC90 we come across, I vote we take its wheels and use them. If I go over anything with that on, I think it'll just fall off."

"Yes, mate," replied Shawn, "In that case let's not use all the bolts, so it's easier to remove." As I was holding the panel for Shawn to re-fix the first bolt, I heard a shout.

"Watch out, they're coming out of the woods." This was followed by bursts of fire. I had to trust that they were capable of dealing with the new threat, and carry on fixing the car. We couldn't move until we had, so my going to see how great a threat it was would not help, only slow us down. If they needed us, I was sure they'd soon let us know.

The increasing volume of fire and shouting from the other side of the trailer made concentrating on the bolts a difficult job. Trying to speed up only made the job slower as we fumbled, dropping bolts and nuts in our haste.

Stuffing the spare bolts in his pocket, Shawn declared, "That'll do for now. Let's get out of here."

We grabbed our weapons and ran around to the other side of the trailer. Half of the group, including Becky, stood in a line firing at zombies that were emerging from the woods adjoining the motorway, the corpses piling up at the hole in the fence made by a crashed car that had smashed into a tree.

I got Dave's attention by tapping him on the shoulder. "Finished?" He shouted over the firing. At my nod, he shouted to Simon in the trailer.

"We're pulling back, cover us from up there." And then to the others in the line, "One by one, peel off and get into the trailer."

From only one day of training, the discipline was impressive. Everyone held their nerve and waited until told by Dave to leave the firing line. Knowing it would not take me long to climb into the car, I joined the line, with my rifle held ready, prepared to fire if necessary.

Shawn climbed into the tractor and started the engine.

"Tom, go and tell the others to start boarding, and then get your car started.

Covered by fire from everyone in the trailer, Dave was the last one to leave the line and climb the ladder to get into the Volvo. Sitting down heavily in the seat, he drank deeply from a bottle of water.

"We cannot keep getting in these situations. They're not like a normal enemy, they don't know what retreat is, and don't care how many we've killed. All they do is keep coming until there are no more of them or they've got you.

We simply do not have enough ammunition to keep fighting like that. I know we had to then, due to unforeseen circumstances. Unless we can avoid it, we're going to have to pick our fights carefully or find a shit load more ammunition."

Driving the Volvo was made even harder by the narrow 'get me home' tyre, but we were moving again and that was the main thing.

With the day wearing on, so did the distance to go reduce. We found a Volvo on an empty stretch of road, and a quick check confirmed the rims were the same as mine, but the only barrier to getting them was the family of four still trapped inside. None had any sign of an injury, so they must have turned at the same time.

Dealing with the occupants took me back to the very start of the event, when I'd met Shawn in those first desperate few hours escaping from St Agnes.

Holding my knife ready, I opened the passenger door. The woman trapped by the seatbelt snarled and snapped her teeth, her arms trying to reach me. I stepped back out of her line of sight, and she quietened down, moving her head from side to side in her effort to locate me again. Shawn then banged loudly on the driver's side window. Her head immediately looked towards the new sound. I took one pace forward and stabbed her through the ear, killing her again.

The glove box, where I hoped the locking wheel nut key was kept, was now accessible. It was there. Despite being no danger to us now, Shawn insisted we put down the rest of the family in the car.

His zombie mantra of 'kill everyone you can, because, if you do not, that one will be the one to get you' did make sense, and no matter how many millions of the undead were now roaming the British Isles, a few less was still a few less.

The banging on the window routine worked for the others too. The father and two sons soon joined their mother in hopefully a more peaceful place.

Lifting the car up with the tractor bucket made removing the wheels an easy job. With a few zombies making their way towards us, we lifted the wheels into the tractor's bucket and drove on to find a better place to swap my wheels over.

The motorway was completely blocked at the Weston-super-Mare junction. The accidents and ensuing chaos had no doubt been caused by the thousands of holidaymakers desperately fleeing danger, only to become part of the problem themselves when trapped by an impassable roadblock. They'd have been unable to return against the tide of people still trying to leave, falling victim to either a virus carrier or one who had already turned.

From a distance, it was clear the way ahead was impossible to negotiate due to the number of vehicles involved and the thousands of undead, who I could see through the binoculars, milling aimlessly together, waiting for their next meal to appear.

I checked the map to find one of the alternative routes we'd planned. After a quick radio check with Shawn, we turned around and headed back to the previous exit, where we hoped we could use minor side roads to circumvent the crash.

The sides roads were clear, thankfully, and we soon navigated our way back to the motorway and continued north. We were almost there when Louise's voice came over the radio.

"There's somebody approaching, it looks like army trucks." Curious, I pulled out from behind the tractor, so I could see ahead.

In the distance, heading towards us on our side of the carriageway, I could see what appeared to be an army convoy.

"Let me deal with this," Dave said, "We don't know what they've been through or who's leading them. Keep your guns out of view, we don't want to spook them."

The convoy slowed as it approached. There were six vehicles led by an armoured vehicle with a machine gun turret on top, and behind it were three lorries and two land rovers. Dave stood up, making himself as visible as possible and raised his arm in welcome. The convoy stopped, and menacingly, the machine gun turned to point in our direction. From my position, I couldn't see anyone in the trailer, but I hoped Simon had the sense to tell everyone to keep their guns hidden.

The door on the armoured vehicle opened and a soldier stepped out.

"That's the first good news," Dave whispered. "They have an officer in charge. I'll go and have a chat."

He lowered the ladder and walked over to the officer. He came to attention and saluted smartly. The officer returned the salute and then extended his hand to shake Dave's. I could feel the tension dropping from me.

The two soldiers talked for a few minutes until the officer turned and issued a command through the vehicle's open door.

Soon after that, doors opened on all the other vehicles and soldiers stepped out. Under the command of what I assumed was a sergeant, they spread out to provide perimeter security. My last worries were dispelled when I saw they were all looking outwards with their weapons ready, and not looking towards us.

Dave turned and shouted, "It's okay, everyone. Do you all want to come down and meet Captain Hammond?"

Once I'd helped Becky and the kids down from the trailer, giving them each a quick hug, we all gathered around the captain. Dave introduced him, and he then told us what had happened to him and his men since the outbreak started.

They were based at Imjin Barracks near Gloucester, where they formed part of the Allied Rapid Reaction Corps that was based there.

In the chaos of the first morning of the outbreak, they were issued with the same orders that every unit must have been given around the country: To go out and quell the public unrest that had broken out seemingly everywhere.

Captain Hammond and his unit soon found themselves fighting for their lives amongst the streets of Cheltenham. His emotions showed when he told us how he and his men had to watch their comrades and friends being ripped apart by the ever-advancing mob. They worked out the hard way that the only way to kill them was to aim for the head, but for many, this knowledge came too late. The young Captain could hear, amongst his own desperate calls for support on the radio, many other units pleading for orders and help. As they fell silent, one by one, he realised help was never going to arrive and his only priority was to lead his remaining men to safety.

Using their scant knowledge of the town, they fought their way through the streets and back alleys of Cheltenham, all the time heading in the general direction of their base near Gloucester.

Exhausted and running low on ammunition, they found themselves surrounded by a huge crowd of zombies. They had no choice but to seek shelter in a house and barricade themselves in. Their location soon became surrounded by the undead and their sanctuary became their prison. From his unit of forty men, only fifteen, including himself, had made it.

Unable to contact anybody on their radios, they were stuck. For days they could do little else but watch as the undead claimed the town from the living. Fortunately for them, the fires that burnt fiercely in other parts of the town were fanned away from them by the wind.

Out of food and with the water supply stopped, they were running out of options until today when they looked out of the window and saw that the mob that had been surrounding them had moved on during the night.

Seizing the opportunity, they immediately left their prison of the last few days and force marched back to their barracks, using all of their training to avoid the wandering crowds of zombies, and hoping to find some sort of authority left for them to report to.

The base was guarded only by the undead. From his description, it sounded very similar to Bickley. Most of the zombies had moved on in search of their next meal, as there was no one living, so nothing was left to keep them there.

During their enforced incarceration, they'd already planned and discussed many different scenarios, should they ever be able to escape. They were soldiers in a rifle regiment normally based in barracks near Exeter, so the only aim for most of them was to try and get back home to find their families. The young Captain decided that as there was no command structure he could contact, his loyalty and duty was to his men.

Imjin Barracks was the Headquarters for the Allied Rapid Reaction force, so it was well equipped with a wide variety of military equipment and ordnance suitable for a whole range of military campaigns.

Scavenging more ammunition from soldiers who had turned, and from bodies of their former comrades littering the base, they cleared the base of any threats. Then selecting vehicles from the motor pool, they broke into the Armoury, loaded the vehicles to capacity and headed south.

The soldiers all looked at the end of their endurance, their exhausted faces, drawn and haggard. Only training, discipline and the need to reach their families was keeping them going.

Captain Hammond then listened as we gave him a quick résumé of our last few days and why we were heading north.

He asked questions about the route south. The relief showed on his face, when he and his sergeant looked at the map Shawn produced to show him the routes we had taken to avoid the crashes, and he knew they could make it to Exeter.

The news that the route north as far as Gloucester was passable filled us with new hope that we would make Bristol before night fell. As we had, they had cleared a route through blocked parts using the power of the lead armoured vehicle, only having to leave the motorway at one point, which they showed us on the map.

Studying our vehicles and the adaptations we'd made, he was full of praise for our ingenuity and the steps we'd taken to survive. There was a tense moment when he looked serious and said,

"As the ranking officer, I could order you and your men to come with me."

Pausing as he looked at our shocked faces, he then smiled wearily, "But I guess you would refuse and that could place us in a tricky situation, so for what difference it makes, I order you to continue helping these civilians and help them to reach their destination." Both Sergeants saluted the officer and accepted his orders. Dave then asked him a question with a slight grin on his face.

"Sir, as we are now following orders, can I request a resupply of ammunition? You've told us you're fully loaded. We could do with more, so we can complete our orders."

"Don't push it, Sergeant!" Simon intervened.

"We can always trade, sir. I'm sure we have items you need."

"As an Officer, I cannot engage in trade of Government-owned property." He turned to his Sergeant. "But the sneaky man by my side, I assume knows how these things work when his officer's back is turned." He then stepped six inches to the side and looked innocently around. With a grin, the Sergeant looked at Dave and Simon.

"Right mates, as my commanding officer is currently indisposed, what have you got and what do you need?"

"We have food," Dave replied, "hunting rifles chambered for .556, which we've found make great sniper rifles, so you can reach out and touch things from a nice safe distance. And if you want them, plenty of shotgun cartridges. I can even throw in a few shotguns to sweeten the deal if you want.

What we need is as much .556 as you can spare, and if you have anything heavier that would be useful." The Sergeant glanced at Captain Hammond, who nodded slightly.

It was not really a negotiation and both sides knew that, but for some reason, probably drilled into the soldiers from the years of surreptitious deals that kept the British Army better supplied and fed than regular channels did, they haggled briefly until striking a deal.

We gave them half of the food in the rear of my Volvo, five rifles, five shotguns and a few thousand cartridges in exchange for a pallet of .556 ammunition, a few boxes of grenades, and two light machine guns.

It was fantastic, from a chance meeting with the only other group we'd met so far, we'd gained enough ammunition to fight a small war, along with some extra weaponry that would provide a lot of extra firepower.

While the ammunition was being handed up to the trailer from one of the lorries that had backed up to it, Dave told the Captain about Willie and gave them the location of his farm as a good place to head to when they found their families alive. It was left unsaid that it would also be a good place to go if they were not.

Both parties were eager to continue their separate journeys as soon as the last exchange items were loaded.

It did seem wrong, leaving the first survivors we had come across, but we had separate but similar goals. They needed to find their families as did we, but they did know where we were heading to, and the Captain said that if they couldn't find a safe place to shelter once they'd rescued their families, then they would most likely try for Warwick castle.

As we parted, I genuinely hoped we would see them again.

The cleared route enabled Shawn to maintain his maximum speed. The momentum made it easy for the plough to carve through and destroy any zombies in our path. Bodies were sent flying, cartwheeling through the air or just disintegrating when hit by the solid sides of the blade.

The tractor slowed as we left the motorway at the exit Shawn had told me we were going to take. My anticipation and nervousness built, knowing his house was only a few minutes away.

Spears were used again as we drove down streets empty except for zombies. Shawn was driving as fast as he could. He'd been waiting days to see if his mates had survived, and now he was only minutes from finding out.

Louise's voice spoke through the radio. "Shawn's road is the next on the left." I craned my neck forward, eager to see anything at all. He started to turn in to the road and stopped. His voice came over the radio. He sounded excited.

"There's a crowd of them outside my house. They have to be in there."

I could see a bus and a van a hundred yards away outside a house. Hundreds of zombies were filling the street, pressing against the sides of them.

Dave beside me, lifted up the machine gun we'd obtained earlier. He pulled back the charging handle and lifted it to his shoulder, testing the weight.

He shouted so everyone in both the car and the trailer could hear.

"Everyone, we've done this before. Keep your fire away from the house and pick your targets." He picked up the radio.

"Shawn. Stop as close to those vehicles as you can. We'll be right behind you."

Not needing to be told twice, the tractor lurched forwards, accelerating down the street, bodies cascading as the plough burst through the mass of undead.

The second he stopped, rifles appeared over the side and began firing. Dave used controlled, aimed bursts from his machine gun to pour a massive amount of lead at zombies' heads, which disappeared in showers of blood and bone every time he pulled the trigger. At every boom of a shotgun or crack from a rifle, another zombie fell until eventually the road was carpeted with mutilated, smoking corpses. Some inevitably still twitched and thrashed, but they lay so deep, even the ones that had not been hit were trapped under ones that been killed.

The firing slowed as the number or targets decreased, until eventually Dave shouted.

"Cease fire!"

The road had turned into a sea of carnage. The damage we'd caused in a short time was horrific. The nearest bodies, hit many times, were unrecognisable lumps of smoking meat.

But we had done it.

Against all the odds, a group of strangers had joined forces and journeyed more than a hundred miles, fighting together to overcome terrifying, bowel-loosening moments. But we'd also formed strong bonds and still had the ability to laugh together, despite the world around us falling apart.

The door opened on the house. Shawn, standing on the wheel arch of the tractor, called out.

"Ian, Dave. It's Shawn, are you okay?"

At the sound of his voice, the door fully opened, and we gawped as seven knights wearing full armour and holding a variety of swords, axes and a mace, stormed out.

"Shawn?" said one of them. He was huge.

"Ian. Yes, mate, it's me." He rested his axe on his shoulder and looked at him.

"Well you took your bloody time, didn't you? And why the hell did you turn up now? I was just about to win Scotland from Dave and become the undisputed Poker champion of the world. And you just turn up and ruin it. Cheers, mate."

Shawn crossed his arms. "Are you drunk?" Ian looked at all the faces staring at him and looked sheepish.

"No. I'm a lot more sober than I was an hour ago. That was when we ran out of whisky." Maud stopped any more talking. Her angry voice stopped them in their tracks.

"Can you two fools stop it? I have a baby who needs feeding and four children who need the toilet. Now stop your tomfoolery and find a way for us to get down from this infernal trailer." We used our ladder to climb up into the trailer and then helped each other climb over to the roof of the bus and down a ladder we put on the other side.

One by one, everyone trooped into the house. The living room was large, but it was full to bursting when the last one squeezed in. Shawn was overjoyed at finding his friends all alive and in one piece. We watched, smiling as the friends hugged, laughed with sheer joy and clapped each other on the back.

When the reunion had calmed enough, Shawn introduced us to his friends.

We were now thirty, and a dog.

EPILOGUE

Tom and his family and friends, successfully united with Shawn and his friends, were at last one group. The celebrations gave way eventually to the reality of their continued struggle to survive, and the wider concerns and hopes of finding other survivors. They still had family of their own to search out, and friends whose fate they knew nothing of. The fear that the virus had turned most of the world's population into zombies was very real.

They knew that so far, luck had been on their side, but there was no knowing how long that would continue. Another very real concern for them was that they might lose members of their group to the horrifying hordes of undead that plagued their every move.

As they began to plan the next stage in their journey, the uppermost thought in their minds was of who else might still be surviving in the desolation the plague had created. The one hope that had kept them together was to reach the sanctuary and safety that Warwick Castle might provide.

Chris Harris is a UK-based author, well-known for his post-apocalyptic and zombie book series.

Find his website at www.chrisharrisauthor.co.uk

Facebook @chrisharrisauthor

UK Dark Book 1: The Blackout

By Chris Harris

"What would happen if……?"

Many people ask themselves the question, but how many actually do something about it?

Tom lives in Birmingham, England with his family. After asking himself the question and researching what could happen, he decided it wouldn't do any harm to be a little bit prepared. Just in case.

He discovers the world is going to be hit by a massive Coronal Mass Ejection from the sun, which will turn the whole planet dark.

He only has a few days to get ready.

Will they survive?

People want what they have, but is he prepared to kill to protect it?

The UK Dark series, out now!

www.ingramcontent.com/pod-product-compliance
Lightning Source LLC
Chambersburg PA
CBHW032126170626
46808CB00006B/2124